# The Ten-Cow Wives' Club

ALSO BY
JONI HILTON:

*The Best Kind of Mom*

*The Power of Prayer*

# The Ten-Cow Wives' Club

*a novel*

## Joni Hilton

Covenant Communications, Inc.

To all the women in my own Ten-Cow Wives' Clubs

# Prologue

*A friend loveth at all times . . .*
Proverbs 17:17

It's nighttime, and I'm sleeping over at Tanya's house. It's a balmy summer night, so we're out on the back porch where the crickets sing and the moths flutter against the golden porch light. We're both in the third grade, and today I was baptized. Tanya is asleep in a concoction of quilts and blankets, while I'm snuggled down into my brother's sleeping bag from a million Scout camps.

I look over at my sleeping friend. Her hand is limp, her fingers curved against her pillow like stair steps for a fairy. Stars look down, a cloud stops and tangles itself in the knotted branches of an old oak tree, and somewhere a dog barks. This is our neighborhood: the sidewalk cracks we've memorized, the moms we know like our own, the pajamas we share, the blue cereal bowls waiting in the cupboard for us to fill them up tomorrow. I even know the spoon I want, in the back of Tanya's drawer.

I press my fingers to my thumbs. They didn't wrinkle in the baptismal font today, but somehow I think they'll be wrinkled now, if only because I've thought all day about my baptism, the water closing in on me as my dad lowered me down, the rush of light and splash as I came back up, and the brightness of the room when I opened my eyes again. I'm too excited to sleep.

I look over at Tanya again, and wonder if she felt the way I did when she was baptized. Did she feel like she was falling up? That light was pulling her the way a magnet would? That water and light mixed in motion, never holding still, but casting prisms into the air?

In an eerie but clear instant, I feel she has missed that. I will not embarrass her and ask her about it in the morning. Instead, I vow I will be there for her all her life. I will help her find the magic, the swirling warmth within her chest, the calmness and brightness all at once. I am eight years old, and I love my dearest friend. I will help her, and I will never give up.

# Chapter 1

*Thou shalt live together in love . . .*
D&C 42:45

Maxine always orders dessert first. If anyone ever questions this, she always says the same thing. "What if a meteor hits? I'll have missed the best part!" Maxine is our role model. She knows life was meant to be lived with passion and pizzazz, and wouldn't consider saving her best china or her best nightgown for some special occasion. "You never know when the Second Coming will be, so always look gorgeous."

I think of this as I shlub around in a sweatshirt and a pair of jeans, taking the kids to school, cleaning, cooking, gardening, working on my Sunday School lesson, *maybe* exercising, and squeezing in a few errands before I have to pick them up again. *How would Maxine do this?* I wonder. First of all, she'd do it in a glamorous pair of high heels, dangly earrings, and her seventy-five-year-old body which would put me to shame right there.

Maxine is the "token senior," as she likes to call herself when ordering lunch. "I'm the one who makes the math hard when we're figuring out the bill." She is also the woman we all want to be when we're her age—youthful, energetic, elegant, and just a little feisty. And she's probably the coolest one in the bunch, even at twice our ages.

Widowed twenty years ago, Maxine is still the epitome of a devoted wife. "I talk to Sam all the time," she says, matter-of-factly.

"I tell him how our stocks are doing, how the nieces and nephews are growing up, how ridiculous television has become, and to eat his vegetables. And, of course, I remind him that I'm on my way, and he'd better be planning a huge welcoming party!" She's the one we'd run to if we were ever to lose our own husbands. Maxine would somehow get us through.

"You have to know the gospel," she once said when someone asked her how she could be so happy. "This life is a blink." She snapped her fingers. "Sam and I will be back together before you know it. Thank goodness I chose a good man," and she winked, "and then made him even better. I can't wait to see him again."

If any of us complain about our husbands or our marriages, Maxine always seems to know how to solve the problem. Invariably she includes with the advice her ancient, but still true, wisdom. "You find a way to admire and adore him," Maxine says. "Do more for him. Treat him like a king. He won't abuse it; he'll honor you as his queen. You do it for one week and let me know what happens." Sure enough, Maxine's seemingly old-fashioned advice always seems to work. "Have you been to AA?" she'll ask, her wrinkled hand on one of our arms. Of course, she means Admire and Adore.

Tanya's the only one who ever bristles at Maxine's relentless cheer. "Life is not a Hostess cupcake," Tanya once said, lowering her chin to look over her leopard-print sunglasses at the older woman. "It's far more complicated than that."

Maxine cocked her head, pretending to actually think about it. But then, "Not really." She smiled. "It's pretty much a cupcake."

Tanya smirked. "And how is that?"

"Well," Maxine explained, "you've got the curly icing on the top, which is really just a facade, not a true picture of what's under it. That's like dating."

We all laughed, and she went on. "Then you've got the cake itself. It can be kind of dry, a little messy, a little crummy." Maxine grinned. "Those are the struggling years in a marriage. Then, if you work your way through the cake, you find the delicious creamy center, pure and sweet."

"You're making me gag," Tanya laughed. "Cupcakes as a metaphor of life now."

Maxine shrugged. "You're the one who brought up cupcakes."

Tanya shook her head and went back to her Thai salad. Tanya has been eating Thai salads at our luncheons for four years now, trying to lose weight. What used to be curves and flourishes have filled into bulges and sags like on the rest of us, and Tanya is fighting genetics and gravity, trying to get her teenage figure back. Today she had her dark hair slicked back into a tight knot at the base of her neck.

"You guys have it easy," she said to the rest of us. "You don't need a hunter body." Tanya was divorced ten years ago, and has tried every diet, every get-young-quick cream, and every anti-aging pill that comes along.

"Every year, there's a new batch of coeds stealing all the great guys," she lamented. "I have to compete with younger and younger women." Tanya watches glumly as men her age fall for women in their twenties and early thirties. She spends an hour at the gym five days a week, and reads about plastic surgery on the other two.

"I'm telling you, any guy worth having will want someone his own age. He won't look twice at some young . . ." Ships groped for adjectives. "Some young, firm, pretty, small-waisted . . . I'm not helping, am I?"

Tanya laughed. "Thanks for the comfort."

Ships is the nickname we gave Wilma Shipley, who begged us in the seventh grade not to tell anyone her first name was Wilma. "It isn't just the name," she said. "It's that I have red hair—people will call me Wilma Flintstone." So we made a pact and called her Ships forever after. She, Tanya, Crystal, and I all went to high school together in Tracer City. We have the wonderful fortune that we all now live in the Bay Area, so we can still meet for lunch every month. Years ago we added Maxine, who lived in my ward and felt like a kindred spirit the minute we met her.

"Why can't you just be happy by yourself?" Maxine asked.

"Because I can't," Tanya said from between her teeth, and then pretending to collapse in a heap. Tanya had always wanted to be an actress, so we expect a certain amount of drama-queen behavior from her.

"Here," Ships said, gesturing at the cute waiter. "Marry him and shut up."

Tanya smirked. "Maybe I'll just do that."

"Maybe you just should," Ships said.

Soon they were flicking ice water at each other until I leaned over the table and grabbed both their wrists. "Children, children," I said. "No food fighting in the cafeteria."

Tanya sighed. "I know I seem obsessed with remarrying," she said. "But I'm still young, you know?"

We did know. Inside every woman is a twenty-year-old ingénue. We never tire of compliments, romance, gifts, or attention. We all remember the names of our dolls. The little girl in us stays right there under the surface, still smiling at puppies and kittens, still closing our eyes when we inhale a new fragrance, still excited to get dressed up for a special occasion. And I hope that never changes, no matter how old we get.

# Thai Salad

1/4 cup lime juice
2 Tablespoons rice vinegar
2 Tablespoons Thai fish sauce
1/2 teaspoon red pepper flakes, crushed
1 Tablespoon sugar
1 Tablespoon canola oil
2 Tablespoons fresh cilantro, chopped
2 cups mango, chopped
1 red bell pepper, diced
1 1/2 lbs. bay shrimp, cooked
4 cups lettuce greens
8 basil leaves, chopped

In a jar, combine first seven ingredients and shake well to combine. Tanya shakes it a little longer, hoping to burn calories. Pour into a large bowl with mango, bell pepper, and shrimp. Chill 1 hour. Toss with greens and basil.

Serves 6.

(Tanya would never do this, but you can add 1/2 cup chopped peanuts if you're not watching your weight.)

# Chapter 2

*Learn wisdom in thy youth . . .*
Alma 37:35

I can still hear the film clicking through the projector in seminary. It was the late sixties, before everything was on video, and Brother Jamison was fumbling in the dimly-lit room, trying to catch the end of the plastic ribbon.

We had just watched *Johnny Lingo* and had discovered how the tribe's shy and homely Mahana was transformed into a confident, elegant spokesmodel by Johnny Lingo's clever purchase of her for the unheard-of sum of eight cows. He had established her value to one and all, especially to Mahana herself.

It was a rite of passage, this watching of *Johnny Lingo,* and it made us officially eligible LDS girls. Other people became debutantes and had coming-out parties; we sat there wearing knee socks and penny loafers, watched *Johnny Lingo,* and resolved to be women worth eight cows.

At slumber parties, we'd speculate about who our future husbands would be. It was never anyone from the ward, but some "mystery man" yet to make an appearance.

"I think Ships is going to marry a bald guy," Tanya said. Tanya was a tall brunette with lustrous hair and full lips. She was the most daring and outspoken of our group.

"Am not," Ships said. "Unless he's smart, rich, and debonair." Ships tossed her own auburn hair, grinning confidently around her retainer and through the freckles on her shiny cheeks.

Oh, we had lists longer than our below-the-kneecap skirts. We wanted guys who were tall, blue-eyed, tan, funny, brilliant, honest, romantic, sociable, charming, good father material, hardworking, spiritual, masculine yet tender . . . have I left out anything? Meanwhile, the guys were probably compiling their own wish lists. No, actually, the guys were probably watching a ballgame. But we knew they'd eventually get around to the serious business of picking a bride, and we wanted to be fully qualified.

We cooked, canned, sewed, crocheted, embroidered, gardened, babysat, and blew our hair dry just so. We shopped for cute clothes, we learned to apply makeup, we memorized scriptures, we did service projects. We studied for every test; we took piano, ballet, and art lessons. We slathered QT on ourselves to get a tan, and ended up looking like giant orange Cheetos. We walked to Woolworth's on Friday afternoons, wearing big plastic curlers, because even if you didn't have a date, wearing curlers meant you did. We were perfectly suited to be plunked into a Jane Austen novel.

Meanwhile, the guys were reading comic books, working on car engines, lifting weights, smacking each other with wet towels in the locker room, and burping the Pledge of Allegiance, just to see if they could do it. It would be years before they would realize the veritable candyland of female treasure into which they had luckily been born. All our years of wearing cucumber facial masks and taking good care of our cuticles was just waiting to be appreciated.

And waiting. And waiting.

I think I was eighteen before I finally got asked out on a date. And then it was by a dweeby kid who used to sit behind me in drivers' ed and kick my chair.

"I don't know what it is with the boys in our ward," Bishop Slater sheepishly admitted to our Laurel group one time. "They just don't want to go on dates. You girls must be planning group activities that are just too fun."

We looked at each other with narrowed eyes. *We've been self-sabotaging?* All these years we've been trotting our party-planning skills out onto the stage of life, and the guys haven't even noticed? Suddenly I pictured a goofy-eyed Great Dane, just lapping up whatever lands in his bowl, without ever trying to determine its source.

Okay, it was obvious that a totally different strategy was needed. In order to outsmart the totally not smart, we would have to think like a guy. This was not easy.

"What do they think about?" Crystal asked. Her blond curls and huge, innocent eyes made her look like a Kewpie doll.

We all shrugged. Even those of us with brothers could only think of three things: food, sports, and rock music.

"We'll never understand them," I muttered. Not that we were against food, sports, or rock music; we just didn't *think* about those things.

It was like trying to date aliens.

Then Tanya got an idea. "Why are we sitting here like lumps, waiting for them to make the first move? Let's ask *them* out."

The chorus of "no's" lasted several minutes, as we brought our friend back to this planet and put an abrupt end to such a crazy idea. That just wasn't done in those days. It would be seen as forward. Nobody wanted to be forward; that was worse than being backward.

But we did think about it.

Finally Tanya decided to lead the way. Naturally, this meant she got her pick of the guys, and chose to ask Dan Avey out for pizza and root beer. Dan Avey was easily the cutest guy in the whole high school, not to mention at church.

And he accepted! We were thunderstruck. Could something so bizarre, so daring, so completely different than the universe had always been, actually work?

The whole ward—okay, the part that mattered to us, the teenage girl part—was buzzing. Tanya was a true pioneer. She deserved a Nobel Prize for discovering a new land.

We all made our plans based on the new information. Of course, some of us were too chicken to ask a guy on an actual date, so instead we planned a party at one of our houses, and asked individual guys to come. This turned out to be too obscure for the guys, though. They didn't get that it was supposed to be a date; they just thought it was another gathering of church kids.

So we tried again. This time we actually invited individual guys to the movies. But our bad luck prevailed. We chose the weekend of a huge Scout campout, so we all got rejected. Tanya remained our idol, as the only one who had actually succeeded in our cause.

Finally senior prom came, and the guys asked us to go with them "as a group." This meant that we had to buy prom dresses, shoes, and boutonnieres, but that we didn't actually have a date, per se. Still, we grabbed at the offer, grateful not to be moping around the house that night, reduced to finally watching Johnny Carson, as the rest of the world carried out their dates.

And that prom was fun. But it was still not the romance we each longed for in our hearts. We wanted to feel in love—to be dizzy with it. To tuck surprise notes into his locker. To look up and see him staring at us with googly eyes. In short, we wanted all that stuff that basically has nothing to do with real marriage, but which everybody wants when they're teenagers.

We wanted a song.

"How are we supposed to listen to oldies one day, and get sentimental, if they never meant anything to us in the first place?" I asked one day. Three Dog Night was playing in the background.

"And what about my neck?" Ships chimed in. "All those years marching in a precision group, and snapping my head to the side, and now it's permanently locked and—"

Here we all chimed in, laughing: "No one ever kissed it."

Ships was laughing herself. "Well, it's true," she said. Ships had been marching in parades wearing a sequined leotard and fishnet stockings for eight years, as a member of the Tracer City Drill Team, and with her red-in-the-sun auburn hair, she always thought she must look fetching enough to catch the eye of *somebody*. We didn't have the heart to tell her that dressing like a fishing lure doesn't always catch fish. It was her dream for a guy to kiss her on the neck. So, whenever we complained about not dating, she always brought up her neck, the sequined uniform, and the marching band.

"I think you have to ride on one of the floats," I said. "Then you wave like this." I demonstrated the queenly wave. "But then your wrist locks. You have to practice a lot to get kissed, I guess."

"Or you have to be Tanya," Tanya said, winking.

We all looked at each other. Then, as it dawned on us what she meant, I screamed, "He kissed you?"

Tanya's poker face twisted into a smirk. "Well, not exactly," she said.

We all groaned.

"Not yet," she said, straightening her posture to look as prim as the advice she was about to give. "You don't kiss on the first date," she reminded us.

"Well I do," Ships snapped. "I mean, I will, if I ever get the chance."

Now we were all laughing, and Tanya drew a bull's-eye on Ships's neck, with a red felt-tip Flair.

"Now when you wash it off, your neck will still look red and your mom will think you really have been kissed," I said.

Ships shoved me, then stuck her chin out defiantly. "What makes you think I'm washing it off?"

Now Tanya was looking into the mirror of her compact, trying to draw a bull's-eye on her lips, with Bonne Bell lip gloss. We all giggled and tried it, too, reminding each other that if you share lipstick you can catch mono.

"Oh dear," I said, smearing pink gloss over my lips. "And then I'll have to stop dating!"

Graduation came and went in a sweaty day of purple caps and gowns, our parents' flashbulb cubes twisting on their cameras as they captured our big day. Relatives came over with big bowls of macaroni salad and pineapple slush, all winking and optimistically predicting that the next big celebration would be our weddings.

And then it was off to college. And finally, the boys caught up. Tanya and Ships went to the state college in Tracer, while Crystal and I went to BYU. Not one of us got the grades we'd earned in high school, and academic probation suddenly became a risk, due to the newfound social nature of our lives. School seemed like an interruption, an intrusion into the much more enjoyable world of dating. We were like sailors on leave, finally seeing what life had to offer.

Okay, we were not exactly like sailors. We were well behaved. We were just busy. We'd had no idea how exhausting it would be to stay up until midnight every night, then catch a 7:30 class the next morning. When faced with the choice between compiling a bibliography for a report or going on a picnic with the latest Mr. Adorable, we hardly hesitated before picking the latter.

It took a good two years for all of us to get over the novelty and wonder of actually being attractive to the opposite sex. But we finally did buckle down, study, and actually decline dates during finals. Our bleary, bloodshot eyes eventually returned to normal, and we even relished school breaks when we could all get together as girls. We didn't mind leaving the boys behind for awhile.

We usually gathered at my house, since I was the last child in my family and there would be no bothersome tweenies bugging us. We'd set each other's hair (tradition), make smoothies (tradition), and try on each others' clothes (new idea, suggested by Crystal after reading an article about doubling your wardrobe this way). And we all smelled like Jean Naté.

"If bread is really good, you shouldn't have to butter it," Ships said, pouring the orange juice as we settled in for a Saturday morning breakfast.

"Oh, please," I said. "The butter is the whole point. Bread just exists to hold up the butter."

"You would eat a glob of butter plain?" Tanya asked.

"I might."

"I dare you," Crystal said.

I promptly nicked the edge of the butter with a knife, and popped it into my mouth.

"Eeew," they all groaned. "Heather ate butter *plain.*"

"Oh, come off it," I said. "You eat more butter than that on one pancake."

We continued to argue about butter, then moved on to margarine, then mayonnaise, then hair conditioner, then hairstyles. All this while sitting there in our bathrobes with squinty, just-got-up faces.

Then the phone rang. "It's Pe-ter," I sang, handing the receiver to Crystal. I thought she must have pulled the eject handle, she got out of her seat so fast. She grabbed the phone and purred, "Hi, honey." The rest of us rolled our eyes at each other.

Peter was a returned missionary, and was definitely on the wife-path. Crystal, with her tiny but darling figure, her Farrah Fawcett blond hair, and her absolute sweetness, had already turned down proposals from three other guys. What most guys failed to realize was that Crystal was even smarter than she was cute, and she wasn't about to marry a guy who didn't take college seriously. Crystal was a chemistry major, wanted a big family, and figured that to send them all to college meant they'd have to earn scholarships. Thus the gene bank had better include some hefty IQ points. This Peter seemed like the perfect candidate. He was strong in his testimony, and a nuclear biologist in training. Once, when I'd heard him say "radio-pharmaceutical chemistry," I had offered him a glass of water.

He was home from school for the summer as well, and kept trying to pry Crystal away from the clutches of her buddies, with a good bit of success. She'd already been to meet his family in Idaho, where she'd learned to make Spudnuts, and had caught up with them again in Disneyland in June. Now it was almost August, and Peter was clearly going through Crystal withdrawal.

"He wants me to come back to the Y early," she said, hanging up the phone. "He misses me."

We all oohed and clucked. "You going?" Tanya asked.

Crystal shook her head. But from her smile, we could tell it was hopeless. She was already mentally packed and on the plane.

The three of us waved her off at the airport a couple of weeks later, and saw the mixed emotions in her father's eyes as he said,

"She must really like that boy." So none of us were terribly shocked when Crystal called with the big news two weeks later: She and Peter were engaged.

"You're the first one to fall," Tanya teased. "I thought it was going to be Miss Hotpants here." Tanya glanced at Ships.

Ships grabbed the phone from Tanya and said, "We are so excited for you, Crystal! This is just fantastic! When's the big day? Have you picked a dress? What does your ring look like?"

"Somebody needs to invent a way for all of us to talk at once," I whispered to Tanya.

She shrugged. "It'll probably be Peter."

Finally Ships let me pry the phone from her grasp and offer my own congratulations. Twenty suddenly seemed so young. I found myself saying, "Are you sure you want to do this?"

"Yes, mother." Crystal laughed. "He's wonderful! He's everything I've ever dreamed of!"

"Okay, we're all going to throw up now."

Crystal laughed again. "Heather, I told Ships I want all of you guys to be my bridesmaids."

"I'd love to," I said, thinking, *Please don't pick an empire waist dress—we'll all look pregnant.*

"I've already picked the cutest dresses," Crystal cooed. "They'll be red for Christmas, with snowflake lace trim."

*So far, so good . . .*

"And empire waists," Crystal said.

"Ooh," I said, trying to sound pleased. "That sounds just . . . perfect."

"Doesn't it, though?"

And that's how we ended up forming a conga line of Red Hot Mamas at her reception, sticking our stomachs out and posing for a hilarious photo of the four of us, one looking like a demure little bride, and the other three looking like labor-room escapees who'd had the poor taste to wear bright red maternity gowns to emphasize our girth.

Ships was the next to wed, jumping headlong into motherhood by marrying a dashing young widower from Italy, who swept her right off her feet and into the temple. Marco had married in Venice, and had two children with his wife. Her sudden death from a stroke had made him look into religion, and he'd joined the Church. Later he'd decided to move to the United States, where Ships took one look at little Gino and Francesca, and fell in love. It didn't hurt that Marco had that irresistible accent and a boyish shyness that held Ships like a magnet.

She, too, asked us to be her bridesmaids, and stuffed us into ruffled pink gowns that made us look like oversized baby dolls. "Tell me the truth," I said as we went to our fitting. "I look like a blob of cotton candy, don't I?"

"No," tiny Crystal said, pursing her lips. "More like a stack of donuts." Was that supposed to be a compliment?

Poor, busty Tanya looked as if she had helium balloons beneath her bodice, about to lift her away. "I'm thinking of the ugliest outfits in the world for you guys to wear when I get married," she teased. "Just to get even."

But we got through it and managed to have photos taken without an extra-large lens, and only one verse of "We Welcome You to Lollipop Land."

"I am living an absolute fairy tale," Ships reported at our luncheon after their honeymoon—*with* the children. "I love those kids. Marco is incredible. And he cooks all the meals!" Best of all, Marco was an importer, so he could live anywhere, which meant Ships could stay near her family.

"Does he kiss your neck?" Tanya asked.

"Certainly does," Ships said, no hint of shyness about her.

"Okay," I interrupted. "Too much information."

"Heather's always the prude," Tanya said. "I say we hear a full report."

I was saved by a waiter holding four plates and saying, "Chicken salad?" as he set my lunch down before me.

"Mine's the ravioli," Ships said, now unable to eat anything but Italian.

"Shrimp pasta?" the waiter asked.

"Oh, right here." Crystal raised her hand. "It looks wonderful."

"Then the enchilada must be you," he said, plunking Tanya's order in front of her.

"Yep, I'm the enchilada," she deadpanned. "So, back to Marco's kissing—"

"Anyone need any ketchup?" the waiter interrupted.

"Oh, I think we're fine," Crystal said politely.

"Back to Marco," Tanya said, a little louder.

Ships giggled. "Should I tell you?"

"Fresh ground pepper, anyone?" the waiter asked.

Tanya turned toward to the poor waiter and growled, "No. No pepper, no ketchup. We're about to hear about Ships's love life, here—"

"Tanya, stop!" Ships was squealing and laughing, trying to stuff her linen napkin into Tanya's mouth.

"I'd like some pepper," I said, smiling right at Tanya and enjoying her agony.

"You never get pepper!" she snarled, as the waiter obediently twisted the wooden grinder over my salad.

I smiled. "I know."

"Okay, stop it," Tanya said. "Stop with the pepper, already, and shoo. We have things to discuss."

The waiter was blushing now, and hurried off to the kitchen.

"I'm not sure we need to hear every detail of Ships's honeymoon," Crystal offered, diplomatically.

"Thank you," I said. "Some of us have virgin ears."

Tanya smirked, then turned to Ships. "Okay, then just tell me."

"Why don't you just marry that Boston guy and then you'll know all about it?" Ships said.

Tanya sighed. "It's not Boston, it's Preston. Why can't any of you remember that?" She took a huge bite of her enchilada, then waved her hand in front of her mouth and gulped some water. "Hot!" she gasped, eyes watering.

"I can remember him," I said. "I was just talking to Prescott the other day—"

"It's Preston," Tanya said through her teeth. "And I am not marrying him."

"Then why do you care what we call him?" Crystal asked. "I thought it was Westin."

Tanya sighed and shook her head, muttering something about being stuck with pinheads for friends. "I'll tell you who hasn't reported on her love life in some time," she said, glancing my way, "and that's Heather."

I could feel my cheeks warming, and laughed. "That because there's nothing to report." I had gone out with a couple of guys for as long as six months, but nothing much came of either relationship, and I'd wound up using the "let's just be friends" exit. "I am happily in love with fashion design," I said. That was my major at BYU.

They all groaned.

"Where you'll never meet anybody," Tanya said. "Home *Echhh*." She shook her head. "You should major in a guy subject."

I laughed. "I can just see me in medicine, or auto mechanics," I said. "The whole country would stop having operations and car repairs."

"Here is how the world should be," Tanya said. That's been one of her signature lines since the seventh grade. "Guys should work at leotard shops where they'll meet girls, and girls should work at sporting equipment stores, so they can meet guys."

"If we were smart," I said.

"Right," Tanya echoed. "If we were smart."

We hated to break up the luncheon, but we promised to meet for lunch again during the next school break.

That turned out to be in an outdoor café, since Crystal was now expecting and her morning sickness was triggered by smells. We figured a breezy location would be best. We hadn't counted on the pelting rain, but at least we all got there, drenched, and tangling our umbrellas together as we hugged each other.

"I am so jealous," Ships said. "I want to be pregnant, too."

"Hey, you're still ahead of me," Crystal said. "You already have two."

"Gino and Francesca are adorable, I admit," Ships said. "But I do still want to have some of my own, you know?"

"You're both giving me morning sickness," I said. "I cannot even imagine being this young and being pregnant."

"Me either," Tanya agreed. "It's like your whole life is set now."

Crystal smiled. "Set exactly as I want it."

I shrugged. "You're lucky. You met the right guy and the timing is right for you guys to start a family. I'm still figuring out how to work the washer and dryer. I wouldn't even offer to babysit anybody yet."

Tanya was clinking the ice in her glass of water. "I'm not ready to jump into motherhood yet, either. I mean, yes, someday, but . . . I guess you have to find the right father."

"What's wrong with Bronson?" Ships asked.

"It's Preston," Tanya sang, refusing to be pulled in. "And every one of you knows it." She sighed. "He's okay. I don't know. Maybe I'm waiting for fireworks."

"I'm going to finish this semester," Crystal said, "then take off until I can go back to school without neglecting my kids. That might be a long time from now." She shrugged. "But I'll do it."

We knew she would, too. We were all juniors now, and I could almost see the light of graduation at the end of the tunnel.

Ships had opted to do home study, determined to get a degree in accounting, then work part-time from home. "The kids come first," she agreed.

"So." Tanya straightened her glass and silverware, as if conducting a meeting. "Let's hear all about the new baby. We want names, we want size, we want sex."

Unfortunately the waiter approached just as she was listing that last requirement. Tanya froze. The rest of us tried to keep from laughing as the waiter gasped out, "If you're not ready yet, I'll come back in a few minutes." Then he spun around and left before getting an answer.

We were all giggling, and Tanya was holding her head in her hands. "Why do I always do it? I'm always the big mouth."

Crystal was blushing, but took a deep breath and tried to set Tanya's blunder aside. "Well, we've decided not to find out whether it's a boy or a girl," she said.

"That's called gender," I interrupted. "Not sex."

"Fine, fine," Tanya snapped.

"And we won't know the size until it's born. I mean, the doctor can sort of guess, but no one really knows. And as for names, we have no idea."

"So basically, you've reported to this meeting with no information," I said.

Crystal laughed. "That's right."

Then we all bombarded her with names, arguing about this one and that one, until our waiter sensed that the climate had changed and came back for our orders.

"She's having a baby," Tanya told him, trying to explain her previous comment.

"For lunch?" the waiter asked.

We all busted up laughing. "You really should let someone speak on your behalf," I told Tanya. "Bring this poor woman a Caesar salad."

After lunch, we went shopping for maternity clothes and then planned Crystal's baby shower, making sure to include on the invitation that Crystal needed suggestions for names. *Of both sexes,* Tanya wrote. "That's okay, to say that, right?"

Two months later, Crystal was neatly folding the wrapping paper as she carefully untied each gift, surrounded by girlfriends and chatter. "Gimme that," Tanya finally said, snatching one of the gifts and tearing the paper from it in one swoop. "That's how you unwrap a present, dear."

A friend of Crystal's mom was sitting beside me and whispered, "Who is that . . . person who just tore the gift open?"

I smiled. "That's Tanya. We're all kind of like sisters, so . . ."

The woman smiled and nodded. Certain formalities slip away when you've known each other since grade school. Tanya and I went back so far I could remember her saying "sumglasses" and

"Valentimes." Crystal and I had bought our first high heels together. And I recall Ships spitting on her finger and wiping a smudge from Crystal's face, once. And another time, when I was admiring the jacket on a mannequin, Tanya had hissed, "You buy that and I'll kill you." I'd decided not to buy it. Tanya was right—purple and orange stripes just weren't me. (Are they anyone?)

We watch out for each other's diets and allergies, tug at another's bunching sweater, commiserate about our relatives, carry Midol for each other, and feel protective and angry when one of us gets dumped by a guy. The boundary lines between us have grown fuzzy over the years, and we feel a sense of unity with each other. Once the pretenses are down, what's left is four women who can be totally honest and still remain friends. Best friends.

## Idaho Spudnuts

1 pound russet potatoes, peeled and quartered
2 packages yeast (1/4 ounce each)
1 1/2 cups warm milk
1/2 cup vegetable oil
1/2 cup sugar
2 eggs
1 teaspoon salt
7 1/2 cups flour
oil for deep frying
4 cups powdered sugar
1/3 cup water
1 teaspoon vanilla

Boil potatoes until tender; let cool. Make sure they're Idaho potatoes, or Crystal's mother-in-law will come after you. Drain off cooking liquid, reserving 1/2 cup. Mash potatoes. (Crystal would never tell you this, but you can use leftover mashed potatoes, if you like.)

In a large bowl, dissolve yeast in reserved cooking liquid. Add mashed potatoes, milk, oil, sugar, eggs, and salt. Add enough flour to form a soft dough. Place dough ball in a greased bowl, rolling to grease all over. Cover and let rise 1 hour in a warm place, or until doubled. Punch dough down, and let rise again until doubled, about 20 minutes.

Roll out on floured surface to 1/2-inch thickness. Cut with 3-inch doughnut cutter. Heat oil to 375 degrees, and fry a few donuts at a time, until golden brown. For glaze, combine powdered sugar, water, and vanilla. Cool on wire racks.

Makes 4 dozen.

Crystal has to make these on a regular basis, but Ships and I both like to make them on the first day of fall after a long, hot summer.

# Chapter 3

*A virtuous woman is a crown to her husband . . .*
Proverbs 12:4

I graduated from BYU in April 1974, and immediately afterward I joined a group of BYU students to go to Europe for the summer. We had all been saving for years, and had planned our jobs and education around this three-month break.

And it was exhilarating. For me, the art in Florence was the highlight, but I have to say it's pretty hard to top moonlight behind the Eiffel Tower, or mists rolling over Scottish highlands. I wrote home on a postcard, "Died and went to heaven."

My parents were pleased that I had a terrific experience, and Dad, of course, was happy I hadn't found a prospective son-in-law on the trip. The longer I waited to marry, the happier he was. Mom was all for getting my career launched first, as well. She had wanted to be an illustrator when she was young, and even though she had thought she could stay involved in it and raise children, that was an era before creative work-at-home plans. Serious professionals were expected to go to an office. So she had put her drawings on a closet shelf, and never looked back. She always said she was happy she had chosen motherhood, but I knew she kept hoping there would be a way for her own daughters to have the best of both worlds.

My sister, Sarah, took after Dad, and became an attorney. My two brothers, Phil and Mitchell, went into business and real estate.

Only mom and I shared the soul of an artist, and the dreamy notion that everything is possible.

Sarah was a good example of how a career can derail a marriage. She married a fellow law student, and within a year, they were both experts on divorce: their own. She hasn't trusted marriage since. She is now a semiactive Church member with a great career, but no eternal companion. I know my parents' sadness at how Sarah's marriage turned out influenced their advice to me on the subject.

"Do everything life has to offer," my Dad always said to me. "But get to know who you are, first." He actually had a list of things every girl should do before tying the knot, in addition to getting an education: travel, work for a terrible boss, try out for a play, buy your own car, help build houses for the poor in this country or another one, learn to play an instrument, and learn martial arts. He had elaborate reasons for the traits each of these goals would help develop. The only ones I actually did were travel and buy a car. Poor Dad. (On the other hand, I think Sarah actually did all of them, and look where she is now. Go figure.)

The day after I got home from Europe, Tanya got engaged, so naturally we had to meet for lunch as soon as possible.

Preston had finally worn her down and convinced her that a life without him would be a life without acting in the theatre because she'd have to get a steady job. This meant we were all going to have to get his name right, and that Tanya would now become Tanya Towers—perfect name for a marquee if I ever saw one.

"He's so supportive," Tanya said. "He's willing to watch the kids while I do community theatre."

"What kids?" I asked. "You don't even have a wedding dress picked out."

"Well, we're going to start a family as soon as we can," Tanya said.

I felt guilty. The thought of being pregnant gave me jitters, and here were my three best friends rushing blithely into it. I envied their faith.

"Does this look like iced tea to you?" Crystal asked, stirring her root beer and holding it up to the restaurant's dim lighting.

"It looks like watered-down root beer," Ships said. "I'm having spaghetti. How about you guys?"

I turned back to Tanya. "How will you do community theatre if you're always pregnant?"

Tanya shrugged. "I won't *always* be pregnant," she said, nudging Crystal, "unlike our friend here."

Crystal giggled. She had given birth to a beautiful baby boy only a year ago, and now she was expecting another. Tiny Andrew had been the cutest baby any of us had ever seen, and we couldn't wait to hold him and nuzzle the top of his head.

We had all gathered in the hospital waiting room, with "Auntie Ships," "Auntie Tanya," and "Auntie Heather" tags on, screaming and pointing at the little blue-blanketed bundle through the nursery window, until a nurse had to come out and tell us to keep it down.

"Isn't he just precious?" Ships had said, touching the glass.

"Do you think a boy who's pretty will grow up to have, you know . . . problems?" Tanya whispered. We all shushed her.

"Please do not say that to Crystal," I said.

"I won't," Tanya protested. "You think I'm just going to blurt out whatever I think?" After a pause, she added, "Don't answer that."

Finally we were able to see Crystal, who looked like she hadn't even had a baby, and a nurse brought Andrew in for us to see.

"Fresh from heaven," I said, breathing in the glorious smell of newborn babies' heads.

He started fussing, so I handed him back to Crystal, who pulled her hospital gown down to nurse him. "He doesn't quite have the hang of it, yet," she said softly.

"Turn him the other way," Tanya said.

"No, undress him so he can feel your bare skin against him," Ships said.

"Maybe sit up a little," I contributed.

Crystal attempted to do all three at once, and Andrew was getting worked up. "Oh my gosh, now he's crying," Crystal fretted.

"Here. Drink some water," Ships said, handing her a glass.

"Can you just press his lips against you so he can lock on?" My brainy idea.

"The main thing is to relax," Tanya said, punching Crystal's pillows to prop her up more.

Crystal looked anything but relaxed, with the three of us talking at once, fluffing her pillows, and making suggestions based on our own extensive experience.

Finally we realized the commotion of our visit wasn't helping, so we stepped out.

That must have done the trick, because Andrew settled right in.

"Yeow," Crystal said when we came tiptoeing back. "It pinches."

"What are you talking about?" I said. "What pinches?"

"Breastfeeding. It hurts," she said, though still giving her valiant Crystal smile.

"Are you serious?" I pulled up a chair and turned to the other two. "Did you guys know that? Have you heard of this?"

"Sure," Ships said. "Until you toughen up and get used to it. I mean, that's what they say."

"Are you crazy?" I asked. I glanced at the seemingly innocent Andrew. "You do this thing even though it's painful?" I turned back to Crystal. "How much pain are we talking here?"

Crystal's eyes were watering. "Looks like plenty," Tanya observed.

Crystal shook her head. "Don't tell me you've never heard that, Heather."

"How would I hear about it?"

"I guess they teach that in childbirth class," Ships said.

"I bet they don't," Tanya said. "I bet they leave it for a big surprise." She patted me, so I wouldn't feel stupid.

I just stood there shaking my head in amazement.

"What are you worried about?" Ships asked. "We're helping Crystal. We'll help you."

*Oh, good,* I thought. *And we're out here in the hall to give her some peace.* Well, at least I didn't have to worry about it anytime soon. I wasn't even dating any promising prospects. *Maybe, as frustrating as it seems, it is actually a good thing,* I told myself.

\* \* \*

Tanya was still talking about her acting career. "Anyway, I'm planning the whole wedding and honeymoon around auditions."

"You are not." I laughed. "Who would do that?"

Tanya wasn't kidding. "I would do that. And why not? Why should I miss a big break and be miserable on my honeymoon?"

"Have you planned your colors?" Ships asked.

"Oh, I've had that planned for years," Tanya said. "The whole thing—the flowers, the food—it's going to be just like *The Great Gatsby.* You guys will wear pastel yellow drop-waisted dresses—linen, of course, with wide-brimmed matching hats—"

*Hats? Yellow hats? We'll look like dinner mints.*

"And you'll carry parasols. You know, folded up, like canes. We'll have swags of gauzy netting, daisies all over—"

I visualized the whole set, with Tanya in the starring role. I could just shoot F. Scott Fitzgerald. *I hope she doesn't tell us we have to memorize lines.*

But you know what? Tanya actually pulled it off. She created a classy evening, all in pale lemony colors and creamy pearl—wispy and floaty, like a summer breeze over a blue lake. Even the food was dreamy. Tanya, with her dark coloring, looked quite dramatic in that setting, and she seemed never to tire of posing for the photographer.

Preston posed with one hand in his pocket, pulling his jacket back exactly like Robert Redford in the movie. It was to swoon for.

I was glad I wouldn't have to follow a soiree like that anytime soon. For a girl who had majored in fashion design, I was surprisingly unprepared to sketch bridesmaid dresses. Or maybe I thought it would jinx my chances. I resolutely put it out of my mind. But not everyone did.

"So." Crystal was smiling at me over a reception table, and over her nine-month belly. "That makes three of us. Now we just have to get you married off." Luckily I was spared having to think of a response to that, because no sooner had Crystal said it than she went into labor.

"See?" I said, helping her out of her chair. "That'll teach you to meddle with the natural order of other people's lives."

I dashed off to get Peter, and he quickly escorted his wife out of the reception hall.

"Where is Crystal going?" Tanya asked.

I had hoped she wouldn't notice. "She just went into labor," I whispered.

Tanya slapped her bouquet down on a table. "Oh, great. Trust someone to upstage me at my own wedding reception." But she winked, and I breathed a sigh of relief that she was teasing. "Call me in Cancún and let me know what she has," Tanya said.

Ships had also seen Crystal and Peter slip out, and caught up with them in the parking lot to find out what was going on. Soon the whole gathering was buzzing about the pregnant bridesmaid and the incredible timing of it all.

"Hey, maybe that'll be good luck." I nudged Tanya. "Maybe it means *you'll* get pregnant soon." Preston was within earshot, and I saw his neck redden with embarrassment. I hoped he was ready for life with Tanya. My comment was nothing compared to the ones she regularly turned out.

Once when we were visiting teaching companions, we had gone to visit a less-active sister who was, I'm sure, a wonderful person, but who was without a doubt the fattest woman on the planet. No one had prepared us for the gargantuan surprise, and we stammered as we tried to react calmly and sit down in two chairs facing the love seat, which she more than filled. Finally Tanya had blurted, "So. I'll bet you have some killer recipes!" And people wonder why some folks are less active.

As soon as the happy couple left for their honeymoon, Ships and I changed out of our Gatsby dresses and headed over to the hospital. Ships picked up a couple of spinach calzones for us to munch on, in case we had a long wait.

"Did you bring your nametag?" Ships asked.

"Of course," I said, hopping into her Alfa Romeo. "How is our latest nephew going to know who we are if he can't read our tags?" We had baby presents wrapped and ready in Ships's trunk, and sped off.

Then, racing through the doors to the maternity ward, I bumped smack into a man delivering flowers, nearly knocking a spray of mums from his hands.

"Whoa, whoa," he said, grabbing my arms to slow me down and keep from falling. "Where's the fire?"

I looked up to answer him and, honestly, it was the first time in my life that I had felt my knees buckle.

"Huh?" I said blankly, looking up through the flowers. I was sure I looked like a drug addict. He had to be the most handsome man I had ever laid eyes on, and I was actually standing—okay, crumbling—in his arms.

"Are you visiting someone?" he asked.

"Oh, yes," I sighed. Then I smiled up at him, forgetting to add more of an answer.

Ships still had her wits about her. "We're here to see Crystal Wycomb," she explained.

I steadied myself, nodding to Ships's words, and he let me go.

"The waiting room is right there." He pointed to a nearby lounge (which was where we had been heading), and asked if I was all right.

"Uh, blub, I really okay I'll be fine." I smiled. Then I grimaced and looked at Ships for some help.

"I'll watch her," Ships promised, winking and leading me away. She sat me down in a vinyl chair and whispered, "What is wrong with you?"

"Didn't you see him?" I asked.

Ships was just staring at me. "Didn't *you* see him? I mean, you practically knocked him over."

"That was an accident," I said. "But didn't you see how, how . . ." I was looking for the word *gorgeous,* but couldn't find it, ". . . he was?"

Ships laughed. "You are pathetic. You can't see a handsome man without blubbering and going senseless?"

"Evidently," I sighed. "You think he's LDS?"

Ships snorted. "A guy like that? Wearing an Italian suit?" This may have been the first moment when Ships and I shared an identical thought—we both recognized the same designer clothing. Then Ships said, "I think the real question is, Is he single? And the answer is, Fat chance."

She shook her head and went to check with a nurse on Crystal's progress. I just sat there, now completely uninterested in Crystal's progress. I glanced back into the hallway where Mr. Wonderful had been standing only minutes ago. He'd been wearing a turquoise tie that had matched his eyes.

"Pull yourself together," Ships said, coming back to me. "They think she's going to delivery any minute."

I took a deep breath and blinked.

"I have never seen you so gaga over somebody," she said. "You, the one who has always refused to date anyone out of the Church."

"But maybe he's *in* the Church," I said, clinging to the impossible dream.

"And maybe he's a prince," Ships said, mimicking me. "And maybe he'll come and sweep me up onto his white horse, and—"

A door swung open and Crystal's parents dashed in. "Is she in delivery yet?" they asked.

"Soon," Ships said. They sat down by us. "Address all questions to me," she went on. "Heather, here, is useless. She just fell in love with some flower boy in the hallway."

Normally I would have mouthed, "Ships, shut up!" to her, but all I could do was drift back into my blurry world where that man had been holding my arms.

"Oh—I'll bet that was Florence Bench's son," Crystal's mom said, her eyes twinkling.

"Aren't they members—" Brother Spaulding began, but Sister Spaulding interrupted.

"No—you're thinking of the Banks family."

"Oh, that's right. I think he golfs with—"

"Hey," Ships broke in. "Why don't you line him up with Heather?"

My eyes expanded like blowfish. The Spauldings had just said they weren't members, so what was the point? "No! Oh my gosh— you can't call him!"

Sister Spaulding just smiled. "He *is* single," she said.

"I don't care," I sputtered. "I would die of embarrassment."

"She won't die," Ships said. "I say you give him a call."

I yanked Ships aside. "They just said he's not a member. That makes it a completely pointless date!"

"Oh, come on," Ships said. "You can try to convert just one guy, can't you?"

"But—"

My pleas fell on deaf ears because at exactly that moment, the nurse popped in again to tell us Crystal was in delivery. Half an hour later she had delivered another gorgeous boy. Seven pounds, eleven ounces, with fingers as dainty as a doll's.

"He's as cute as the first one!" Ships crowed when we finally got to peer through the nursery windows.

Crystal's parents were dabbing at tears of joy, and went to see Crystal in recovery.

"I can't help feeling a little jealous," Ships admitted after they walked away. "I know I have Gino and Francesca, but I want this experience."

"Yeah, me, too," I said. "The agony, the cramping, the pushing, the mess, then the stitches, and the breastfeeding that feels like you're caught in a vise . . ."

Ships gave my shoulder a playful slap. "You know what I mean."

"Yeah, I know." I put my arm around her. "Your day will come."

Ships hugged me and then grinned impishly. "But if you hook up with Flower Boy, *your* day might come before mine . . ."

I rolled my eyes and laughed. Me as a wife and mother. What a thought.

# Marco's Spinach Calzones

(Add 2 cooked chicken breasts, cubed, to make a main dish.)

1 (2-pound) package frozen pizza dough, thawed
2 (10 ounces) package frozen chopped spinach, thawed
1 cup shredded mozzarella cheese
1/2 teaspoon Italian seasoning
1 can cream of chicken soup
1 egg, beaten

Ships brings these to potlucks and picnics, where they're gobbled up in a hurry. Marco makes his own pizza dough, but Marco doesn't do the laundry, vacuuming, tub scrubbing, or ironing. Therefore, it is okay to use frozen pizza dough. Here's how Marco says to make them:

Cut pizza dough into 8 equal pieces. Pat into triangles, 6 inches per side, on a floured surface. Squeeze water out of spinach. Mix with mozzarella, Italian seasoning, and soup. Divide mixture into center of each triangle, then fold ends into center. Brush dough with beaten egg. Bake on greased baking sheet at 375 degrees for 25–30 minutes.

Makes 8.

# Chapter 4

Ships, Tanya, and I had combined Crystal's and Peter's names into what we thought were darned clever blends of the two.

"Creature," Tanya suggested.

"Pistol," I offered.

But they ignored us and named their new son Christian. Crystal loved the quilt Ships had made, and the little Sunday suit I had designed for Christian. Someday that kid will look back at pictures of himself in a bow tie and beanie, and think, "If I'd only had a set of cymbals, I could have played in a monkey band." But in the meantime, he looked adorable in it.

However, new baby or not, Crystal was the furthest thing from my mind when I came to visit again the following day. My every thought was about finding Mr. Bench, if that was even my mystery man. I was hoping he brought flowers to the hospital on a regular basis.

"You sure I can't get you anything?" I asked, eager for a chance to roam the halls. "From the vending machine, or the cafeteria? How about a magazine?"

"No, I just need to rest," Crystal said. This was a hint of her own, but I was barely listening. "Anyway," she explained, "Peter is due back any second. He'd be happy to get me whatever I might need."

*Yes, but Peter doesn't have the ulterior motive I have.* I thought of saying I might mosey on down to the nursery to look through the windows again, but I decided "mosey" sounded contrived. And it was.

Soon Andrew came toddling in with his father. The boy was too young to really grasp that all his toys were now in danger of getting swiped by a younger brother, and he was smiling from ear to ear.

*The plot has thickened, my boy. You have no idea what all this means.*

I kissed his forehead and tickled his neck, deciding not to trouble him by asking about whether he had looked into safe-deposit boxes. With the arrival of Peter and Andrew, I finally had the perfect excuse to slip away.

Except for two male nurses, everybody on the floor appeared to be female. I went back to the doors where I had originally flown into my dream man. Nothing. I walked down two other corridors, smiling guiltily whenever a technician or nurse went by. Eventually I gave up and went home.

I had lived in dorms and apartments in college, but now I was back at home, looking for work, and wishing I had my own place again. I love my parents, but with so many of my friends living independent lives, I felt too old to be sleeping in my old pink bedroom, which still had pictures clipped from *Seventeen* thumb-tacked to my bulletin board.

I'd finally saved enough money for first and last month's rent, so I sat down to read the classified ads of available apartments.

My current sources of income were twofold: I was an assistant to an interior designer, coming up with window treatments and slipcovers for her (not exactly fashion design, but still working with fabrics), and I was doing fashion photography for local girls who wanted to break into modeling. In a suburb of San Francisco, there were plenty of hopefuls.

Meanwhile, I was still sending out resumes and sketches, hoping to get a clothing line of my own (which is similar to hoping the president will choose you as the national poet laureate).

I circled a few apartment listings, went over to the phone to call them up, and noticed a blinking light on the message machine. I pressed the button.

"Hello, this message is for, uh, Auntie Heather. My name is Jonathan Bench, and, uh, I'm the guy who bumped into you at the hospital the other day. Anyway, sorry I missed you. I'll call again."

I froze. I didn't even dare blink, for fear this was a dream and I'd lose it. Finally my open mouth began drying out, so I closed it and swallowed. "Oh my gosh," I whispered to myself.

Then I panicked. The Spauldings had obviously broken their word—okay, the word I had tried to foist on them—and had told him my number. This was beyond humiliating. Hopefully they hadn't described my absolute lunacy to him.

On the other hand, he'd already seen that. And, even so, he had called.

But, he had called me by that stupid name on my tag, "Auntie Heather." Such an embarrassing attempt to be cute probably looked ridiculous to him.

On the other hand, he had noticed—and remembered—my name tag.

But, he didn't leave a phone number for me to call him back. Probably thought I could become a stalker. On the other hand, he did say he'd call me back.

I listened to the message another five times, hyperanalyzing every word of it, until the phone rang again and I jumped.

"Hi, this is Jonathan Bench," a voice said. It was the same voice, so I knew it wasn't Ships trying to be funny.

"Oh—hi," I managed to say.

"Hi. Do you remember me?"

*Are you kidding?* "I think so," I said.

"Well. Uh, do you like art galleries?"

"I love them." Understatement of the year. You have to be an artist to sketch fashion designs. Art had been my passion since I was scribbling on walls with a magenta crayon.

"Great—a new exhibit is coming to the Pacifica, and I've got a couple of tickets to the opening gala."

"Are you serious?" I bit my tongue. I had been trying to act demure (or at least, not let him hear me panting), but my excitement had gotten the better of me.

"It's next Friday night," he said. "How about I pick you up at seven, we'll grab a bite somewhere, and then head over?"

*Head over heels, you mean.* "Uh, sure," I said. "Yum. I mean, yeah, um, that would be fine." I was slugging my forehead with my fist now.

I hung up, and wiped the sweat off my hands with a paper towel. Maybe I should have apologized for bumping into him, for being so out of it, for the Spauldings giving him my number, for everything dumb I had ever done, but I'd decided not to bring up any of it. We had a date, and I was hanging onto that for dear life. No way did I want to talk too much and make him sorry he called.

But then, of course, I called Crystal and Ships and talked way too much to them. I'd have called Tanya, too, but she was on her honeymoon.

"An art exhibit?" Ships said. "See what I mean? Hey, that's right down your alley—you're going, right?"

"Against my better judgment," I said. "If he isn't LDS, it's about as productive as going out with you guys." Then I caught myself. "I mean, not that going out with you guys is a waste of time, I mean . . . it's just that going out with the girls doesn't lead to marriage."

Ships chuckled. "But maybe this guy will look into the Church, Heather. It does happen, you know."

"Yeah, right," I said. "In like one percent of all cases. I would never hang my hopes on odds like that."

"Okay, so you just go and enjoy the exhibit. He can just be another friend. Like one of the girls."

*Riiiight. One of the girls.* On the other hand, that's pretty much how I treated most non-LDS guys. My brain just couldn't categorize them as possible boyfriends, so I just stopped trying to impress them, and acted the same way as I did with my buddies.

It was even a bit of a relief as I got dressed—I didn't have to get everything perfect, or stress out about my wispy hair. I could just relax and have fun.

When I opened the door, Jonathan held out a bouquet of the most exquisite roses I had ever seen, matched only by the exquisite guy in a tuxedo holding them. I was completely unprepared for either, and I stammered as I thanked him and put the roses in a vase. *This is a waste of a really cute guy.*

As we drove to the gallery, I flipped my visor down to check my lipstick.

"Oh, man," I said, "Don't you just hate it when you start breaking out, right before you have to go somewhere? Then you slather on all this cover-up, and it just looks worse."

Jonathan smiled at me, and I felt encouraged.

"Listen, I really am sorry for plowing into you at the hospital," I went on. "I can be such a klutz sometimes. Oh my gosh—just a week ago I knocked my purse off a chair at this client's house, and let's just say something very personal rolled out! Right at his feet! Wouldn't you know? And he's, like, half bending over to pick it up for me, and half scared to. So I just had to grab it and act like nothing had happened."

Jonathan shook his head. "Sounds pretty embarrassing."

It really was like being out with a girlfriend!

"So what kind of work do you do?" we both asked at the same time, and then we both laughed. I socked him lightly in the arm. "Jinx! You owe me a smoothie."

He raised his eyebrows.

"Oh—I know where we can get the best smoothies—I promise you—that new spa, Luxury? They have a lunch counter where you can just order salads and stuff. I'll take you there sometime. You will love it. Janice did their whole spa. It's full of really soothing greens and aquas, crisp white enamel trim—really looks great. And a little rattan here and there, sort of a Bermuda feel. Ferns, ceiling fans."

Jonathan smiled over at me. "Who's Janice?"

"Oh!" I laughed. "Here I am, rattling along. Janice Premin, the interior designer. I work for her, doing mostly window treatments. I majored in fashion design, so it's kind of related."

"Premin. That sounds familiar," Jonathan said. "Did her mother remarry last year?"

"Yes—do you know her?"

"We did the flowers for the wedding."

"Oh—so you're a florist?"

Jonathan smiled and shrugged. "More or less."

"Don't you just love creating things? I mean, it's so freeing!" I took a roll of flavored mints out of my purse. "Want one?"

"Uh, sure," he said, taking one.

"I love these—my friend, Ships—she was the sane one at the hospital," I winked, "She says they smell too floral—but . . ." I winked again and elbowed him. "We don't mind smelling good, huh?"

"Uh, right," Jonathan said.

He pulled into the parking lot and parked. I hopped out.

"I could have opened your door for you," he said, coming around the car.

I laughed and socked him in the arm again. "Yeah, right. Buddies can just hop out."

He just stared at me.

"Isn't this exciting?" I said. "I love art, and it's so cool to find someone to share that with."

He looked puzzled as we walked in. "This feels odd," he said. "It seems like we've known each other a long time."

I whipped around, my mouth wide open. "Oh, I know! Doesn't it? Like we're old buddies! Oh my gosh—look at that Rémy." I hung on his arm, pulling him over to see an oil of a woman rocking a baby. "You can almost feel the weight of the fabric of her dress," I whispered.

Jonathan nodded, then commented on the lighting. I glanced around the room, wondering if there was anyone there who was actually eligible. Probably not.

"I don't know if the Spauldings told you that I'm LDS," I said, finally. He may as well know the bleak prospects of a relationship, too.

"Yes," he said. "I was glad to hear that."

*What? Oh, great,* I thought. So he would be one of those husbands who's happy to let his wife traipse off to church without him, but while she's there trying to corral the kids, he'll be off boating or playing tennis. He probably thinks he's "tolerant," and will wonder why I'm not equally willing to live and let live.

Or maybe he liked knowing I was LDS, because, let's face it, we do have one or two skills up on our counterparts—I mean, we cook, we sew, we have a sort of old-fashioned appeal.

Well, no matter. He didn't meet the number-one criterion for a romance candidate, and unless he begged to take the missionary discussions by the end of the evening, this one would probably be our last.

A waiter brought us goblets of a decadent concoction he called Chocolate Heaven, and which, after one bite, sent me over to the caterers for the recipe. When I came back, I sat down next to Jonathan at a table near the lounge area.

"Tell me what kinds of clothes you like to design," he said.

Well, that was all it took. I needed no more encouragement than that. I went on and on about the styles I love, the fabrics, the colors, the breezy flow of the lines. He hung on every word. Finally I realized how one-sided I had made the conversation.

"So, tell me about flowers," I said.

He smiled uncertainly. "Heather, do you mind if I—"

I was afraid of this, and jumped right in. "Smoke? Were you going to ask if you could smoke? Oh, please . . ."

Now he laughed aloud, then said, "I do believe this is a nonsmoking gallery."

"You know," I said, "They all should be. Can you imagine how much smoke damage is done to great art in the major museums?"

"They should all become Mormons," he nodded, still grinning at me.

"Well, it couldn't hurt," I said. "Have you ever thought about changing religions?"

"No," he said. "It must be really hard to do. I mean, if you like the one you have, why would you go looking for another one?"

"Yeah." I couldn't help sighing. So that answered that. "So you like yours?"

Jonathan grinned. "I think I'll keep it." He laughed again, then shook his head. "You are so funny."

Just then an Asian couple bumped into us, and Jonathan turned. Automatically bowing, he exchanged words of courtesy with them, in Japanese.

"You speak Japanese?" I asked, as the couple walked away.

"And Spanish, a little high school French." Jonathan smiled. "You?"

"Oh, yeah," I said, purposely exaggerating. "Russian, Hebrew, Swahili . . . I'm pretty much ready for Jeopardy."

"Hey, wouldn't that be something? A Mormon on Jeopardy."

During the drive home I decided that, while Jonathan wasn't really husband material, he was certainly friend material, and I had a sudden idea.

"Hey—you speak Japanese—oh my gosh—I can make tempura! You should come over some night and we'll cook!"

"Uh, sure," he said.

"How about tomorrow?" No need to pretend I have a cramped social schedule with this guy, right? "Unless you're busy?"

He had an amused expression on his face, but said he'd come.

"Bring some sushi; I'll do the rest," I called, after hopping out of his car in front of my apartment.

* * *

Saturday morning the phone rang; it was Ships wanting a full report.

"Oh, he is adorable," I admitted. "But completely out of the question as a boyfriend. He has no interest in changing religions."

"What is he?"

"I don't know. I guess I should have asked. But whatever it is, he's happy with it. I think maybe he smokes."

"Yuck."

"No kidding. But he's a fun friend, so I'm actually seeing him again. He's coming over tonight for Japanese food. If he asks to smoke, I'll have him go out on the balcony. Hey, why don't you come over and meet him? Again, I mean."

She agreed to pop by. Crystal was barely home from the hospital, and Tanya was still on her honeymoon, or I would have made it a whole party.

Jonathan came by at seven with a Japanese-style flower arrangement.

I met him in a kimono. "Isn't this fun?" I gushed, twirling to show him the kimono. "Come in. What darling flowers! Did you arrange them yourself?"

"Well, actually—"

"They'll be the perfect centerpiece," I called back to him, as I placed them on the table. "C'mon into the kitchen and grab an apron," I hollered.

As he tied one of my barbecuing aprons on, I couldn't resist pinching his cheeks. "You are so absolutely gorgeous, do you know that? Honestly, you are the cutest guy in the world!"

Jonathan was clearly flabbergasted, so I socked him in the arm again.

"Oh come on," I teased. "Here. You can chop veggies while I peel the shrimp." I gestured toward a pile of onions, zucchini, mushrooms, and yams.

He started chopping, and I have to admit something: I did want to convert him. I'd been kidding myself; I was wildly attracted to this guy, and my mind was whirling with ways to get him interested in the gospel. At least he already had *some* faith, right? So we could build on that.

"Did you always go to church as a child?" I began.

"Yep. My whole family. You?"

"Yes. My parents worked in a temple, even when I was really young. It's just part of our daily lives, really. That's how a religion should be, don't you think?"

I knew I was pushing it, but then Jonathan agreed. "It ought to be more than a once-a-week commitment."

Oh, hope blooms eternal! This was going perfectly. I'd slowly lead him through the first discussion, then we'd tackle the Word of Wisdom thing, and the next thing you knew, he'd be getting baptized!

Wait—on the other hand, this meant that Jonathan was already very, very involved in his own thing—and, as he had said, not looking for a change.

*Maybe I should try to go for common ground first,* I thought.

"So, it's great to know that God loves us, and that Christ came to earth for us."

"Sure is," Jonathan said. "Do you have a peeler for the yams?"

This was getting even better; the man could cook.

"And a loving Father would want to communicate with His children . . ." I said, angling the discussion toward living prophets, and glancing at Jonathan from the corner of my eye.

"No doubt about it," Jonathan agreed.

I turned around. "Do you ever wonder if God does that? I mean, if he speaks to us in modern times?"

Jonathan squinted. "No, I don't wonder."

Dang. So he's just been led along by some charismatic preacher, and never wondered why we don't still have apostles and prophets to guide us.

"Well, maybe you ought to question that," I said, then smiled, to soften the advice.

Now Jonathan turned to me. "Are you telling me you don't believe God speaks to us today? Sister Spaulding said you were this active LDS girl, with a strong testimony, and now you're telling me to question the authority of the prophet? Are you insane?"

I was frozen with my mouth hanging open.

Jonathan untied his apron and threw it on the counter. "I knew it was too good to be true. This figures . . . I'll bet you've been drinking, too. Just now when you pinched my cheeks—you're drunk, aren't you?"

He was heading for the door now, and I didn't know what else to do, so I screamed.

He turned around.

"Are you telling me you're LDS?" My voice was a squeak. "All this time, you've been a member?"

"What—you didn't know?" Jonathan looked even more confused.

And then it all came back to me—all the intimate comments I'd made, grabbing his arm, things I would never do in a million years with an eligible guy.

"Oh my gosh," I whispered. "All those things I said at the exhibit—"

"You were tugging at your bra," Jonathan said, "and telling me something about the straps—I don't know, I tried not to listen . . ."

I groaned in agony and pulled my apron over my face. "I am so embarrassed. This is the absolute worst day of my life. I am so humiliated. Please forget everything personal I've ever said."

"It was all pretty personal," Jonathan pointed out. "And I'm sorry you don't have as firm a testimony as I was led to believe."

"What?" I brought the apron down again. "You mean you still think I'm drunk? I've never had a drink in my life!"

Jonathan looked at me skeptically. "Normal girls don't just grab your cheeks and . . . wait. So you do have a testimony?"

"Of course! I was trying to convert you! I was sort of doing a first discussion thing . . . sort of."

Jonathan burst into laughter now, and I burst into tears.

"Could you please just leave?" I asked him. "I am terribly sorry and I just want to be alone." I wanted to crawl under my bed for a few hours.

Jonathan leaned against the door, his arms folded, grinning. "Nope."

I dabbed at my tear-streaked face with the apron, and said, "Please go."

Now Jonathan came over to me. "I can't just leave you crying like this."

"No, you could stay and make me cry even harder," I said.

"So this is how you act when you think it's a hopeless case, and you're not really interested in the guy. I'm flattered."

"Hey, the Spauldings said you weren't a member. And then you wanted to smoke—"

"I never wanted to smoke!"

"Yes, you did. You wanted to ask me if you could smoke!"

"*You* said that," Jonathan clarified.

"And then you said you weren't interested in religion—"

"Hold on a second here," Jonathan said. "I am getting misquoted all over the place. I said I wasn't interested in changing. And I'm not."

I sighed, humiliated yet again. "But I thought—well, why did the Spauldings say that?"

Jonathan walked over to my phone and picked it up. "Let's find out."

I gave him their number and he reached Sister Spaulding on the first ring. After some chitchat he said, "By the way, in the hospital, did you mention to Heather that I wasn't a member?" He listened, smiling. "Ah—of the country club. I see . . ." Now he was giving me that same look as he had a few minutes ago when I had jumped to conclusions at the exhibit. Soon he hung up.

"I think I might have misunderstood," I whispered.

"Gee, do you think?" Jonathan was right in my face, now, staring at me with those same turquoise eyes, only they were wide as saucers.

"How could you let me go on and on like that and embarrass myself?" I cried.

"Hey, I didn't know you from Adam. I thought you were just this enthusiastic, uninhibited—"

"Well, I am *very* inhibited, as a matter of fact," I snapped. "Very." I pulled away from him and began pacing. I was frantic that I had said so many inappropriate things. "I am just appalled," I said at last. "It's as if you've been peeking through my diary."

"Hey, you told me every bit of that all on your own," Jonathan said.

"But you went along with it, knowing you were already a member, and didn't say anything—"

"What's to say? I thought you knew. And I went along with it because I'd never met anyone like you before. You were so comfortable with me, so happy. You made me feel . . . like I was home. I had no idea you were thinking I was this smoking nonmember—and why were you dating a nonmember anyway?"

I closed my eyes and summoned patience. "It was Ships's idea. She kept insisting that I could convert you, and I kept telling her no, you were just a friend—"

Jonathan was smiling and shaking his head. "So is that what you want? Just to be friends?"

Now my face flushed purple.

Jonathan came over to me, tipped up my chin, and kissed me. I felt electricity down to my toes. I wondered if my whole kimono had lit up.

"Let me know if you still just want to be friends," he said.

My knees were turning to jelly. "Please forgive me for being such an idiot," I said.

Jonathan smiled. "Please don't change. Don't go back to whatever it is you normally act like around guys. I like the real Heather."

I sighed. "So at least we know that neither of us has a Word of Wisdom problem."

Jonathan laughed.

"I don't usually get things this mixed up," I said.

"That's okay," he said. "I'm glad I wasn't the only one who flipped a little when I saw the cute blond at the hospital."

"I went over there, hoping you'd deliver flowers there again the next day," I admitted.

"Well, that's another misunderstanding," Jonathan said. "I'm not really the delivery guy. I was just filling in for him. I'm a landscape architect and I have a business that includes floral designers.

I was already heading in the direction of the hospital, so I dropped off an order for him."

"That's why you were talking about fountains."

Jonathan smiled. "I design commercial landscapes, mostly. Some private residences. Some Japanese gardens. I went to Japan on my mission."

"Ah . . . that explains . . . I should really slow down, shouldn't I?"

"Be glad they don't give tickets for speeding through life," Jonathan said. "You'd be unable to get insurance."

I could feel the heat in my cheeks again. Just then Ships began banging on the door. "It's meee," she called.

I moaned again and opened the door to a flood of Ships's adventures.

"Oh my gosh," she said, brushing past me into the kitchen, plopping her purse and jacket down on a chair. "You cannot believe the people who can get driver's licenses. I was behind this guy who, I swear, couldn't pick which lane he wanted. He was swerving all over the place. People were honking—which reminds me, the horn on my own car is broken, wouldn't you know, at a time when I actually need it because my life is in danger—and here's this imbecile with a disco ball hanging from his rearview mirror—maybe that's the problem. Maybe he thought he was dancing! I'm telling you, he had to be on drugs."

"Ships!" I managed to break in finally. "This is Jonathan."

"Oh, sorry!" she said, turning to give him a hello hug. "I totally forgot my manners. So are you guys having a complete blast cooking? I am *so* glad you got together. Did you love the art exhibit? Heather said you had the best time—oh—what gorgeous flowers—" Without taking a breath, Ships gave Jonathan a knowing smile and said, "I'll bet you did these, didn't you?"

"Ships—" I desperately tried to break in again.

"So did Heather tell you about our little group? It's just the four of us. Anyway, we've been friends since *forever*, and it's just karma or kismet or something, that we all still live in the Bay Area and can see each other all the time. I'm telling you, it's so therapeutic! Oh my gosh, I don't know what I'd do without my friends, you know? Of course, Heather's the last one still single—" She winked at Jonathan and said, "Maybe you and I can find her the perfect Mormon guy!"

"Ships—" I wondered if I'd have to hit her over the head with a cooking implement to get her to quiet down.

Jonathan was glancing back and forth between Ships and me. I was trying to avoid eye contact with him. Ships kept talking.

"She's so picky, though, you know? I mean, it's good to be particular, but with Heather, it's like the guy has to be—"

"Ships!" I finally screamed. She stopped and looked at me, startled.

"I'm not what you think," Jonathan said into the silence. "I'm LDS."

Now Ships stared at him, then over at me, then back at Jonathan again. "You—whaa?"

Jonathan gave her a nod, almost apologetically.

"Oh my gosh," Ships put a hand over her mouth. "What was I just saying? I thought—I mean—Heather, did you know this?"

I sighed. "Just got the, uh, news," I said.

"Oh, I am so embarrassed. Please forgive me if I said anything inappropriate." Ships was talking even faster now. "I am so sorry—*and* I am due at . . . another place right now, so I'll just run along." She grabbed her coat and fled out the front door, taking her karma and her kismet with her.

"Oh, sure," I called after her. "You can leave."

Jonathan was chuckling and looked at me from his bar stool. I had to admit, his smile was a zillion-watt melting machine. "I wish I'd just had a video running," he said.

I swatted him with a dishcloth.

"And that was just one of the group," I said.

Jonathan laughed. "Are all of you this—energetic?"

"Women talk faster than men," I said weakly.

"Boy, is that the understatement of the year," he said. "How do you carry on conversations with each other?"

I sighed and slumped into a chair. "There's a lot of overlap. As you might imagine."

Jonathan was nodding now, and looked sympathetically down at me, from his higher perch. "I'm gonna make a guess at something."

"Oh, great."

"I'm guessing that, right now, you don't feel much like cooking."

"No, no," I said, rising to my feet. "I can cook. Honestly, it's no troub—"

Jonathan took my hand. "Heather, I want to take you out to dinner. Would you be my date?"

Oh, yeah. Most definitely.

# Chocolate Heaven

In the next life, I think they'll only serve this in the celestial kingdom—another reason to shoot for the top.

1 cup flour
1 1/2 teaspoons baking powder
1/2 teaspoon salt
1/2 cup sugar
1/4 cup plus 2 Tablespoons baking cocoa, divided
1/2 cup milk
3 Tablespoons vegetable oil
1 cup packed brown sugar
1 3/4 cups hot water
vanilla ice cream, optional

Combine flour, baking powder, salt, sugar, and half the cocoa in a large bowl. Stir in milk and oil until smooth. Pour into greased 8-inch square baking pan. Combine the brown sugar and remaining cocoa; sprinkle over batter. Pour hot water over top, but do not stir. Bake at 350 degrees for 40–45 minutes. It makes its own sauce, so serve it in bowls.

Serves 6–8.

# Chapter 5

*Teach the young women . . . to love their husbands . . .*
Titus 2:4

Of course the girls all had a heyday with my blunder. We met for lunch in Sausalito (an emergency meeting called by Ships) to plan damage control.

"This had to happen to our prude," Crystal said, patting my shoulder.

"Tell us everything you said," Tanya instructed.

"No way," I said. "I'm not reliving that much embarrassment."

"You talked about zits, makeup, underwear—what's left?" Ships asked.

I lowered my eyelids. "Look. I am in enough anguish over this already. You guys are not helping matters. I guess I'm not that prudish around other women, but around member guys—I would never have said all that."

Crystal, who had been giggling behind her menu, finally took a deep breath and agreed. "Let's just let Heather solve this one herself," she said.

"Thank you." I closed my menu. "I'm having the chicken tostada and a piña colada shake. What are you guys having?"

They ignored me. "So you actually told him he was gorgeous?" Ships asked.

I sighed.

"And you asked him out—my gosh, I thought I was the gutsy one," Tanya said.

"If you don't pick a lunch, I'm ordering liver for all of you," I said.

"Fine, fine, we're only trying to help," Ships said, studying the pasta section.

"I hate sandwiches," Tanya said. "They wear off all your lipstick. I'll have a salad."

"French onion soup for me," Crystal said.

"How can you eat that?" Tanya said. "I always drip it all down me. The onion pieces are so big! And the cheese is so gooey. But come to think of it, that does sound pretty good . . ."

"So I'm confused," Crystal said. "Are you wanting to see him again?"

"Are you kidding?" Ships interrupted. "She wants to marry the guy!"

"Really!" Crystal smiled. "Our Heather fell hard."

"Yes, well, I fell right into a mud pie," I said. "Never assume anyone's religion, or lack thereof."

"And never ask anyone if they're pregnant," Crystal agreed.

"And never ask anyone if the guy they're with is their son," Tanya offered. She had just made that mistake with a director and his older date.

"And never ask anyone if their kids are really theirs," Ships said. She fielded that question about Gino and Francesca far too often.

"Okay, now we have the rules," I said. "Where's our waiter?"

He materialized almost instantly, and took our orders. "The main thing is," Crystal said, "you guys went out afterwards and had a great time."

"That's right," I said. "Changed out of that stupid-looking kimono and into some slacks and a sweater. Humiliation forgotten."

"By him, but never by you," Tanya said. "I know you're going to suffer over this for years."

"Would you just shut up?" I laughed, tossing a dinner roll at her.

"Hey, who can blame you?" Tanya went on. "I know I'd never get over it either. Think about it."

"She's right," Ships said. "I mean, if you marry him, then this is the story you'll have to tell every time someone asks how you met."

"You're all just so helpful," I said sarcastically. "It really makes me glad I've shared this."

"Oh, you *have* to tell us," Crystal smiled. "It's the law."

"Yeah, well," I said, grabbing back my roll and buttering it, "it's a law that stinks."

"Okay, let's concoct a version of the story that's true, but tasteful," Ships suggested. "You'll just tell people you bumped into him at the hospital."

"That's right. And you did," Crystal said, as if discovering a new fact.

Tanya leaned in, grinning. "But I like the rest of the story better," she cackled. "And that's the one I'm sticking with."

"Fine, you buncha blabbermouths," I said. "You'll be telling the whole world, so I won't have to worry about it."

\* \* \*

If I tried to pinpoint the moment when I fell in love with Jonathan, I could say it was the first time I heard him bear his testimony. Or when I learned that after graduating from BYU he had come back to the Bay Area to care for his ailing parents. Or when I saw his missionary scrapbook with all the smiling children in his arms, and realized what a great dad he would be.

But it was probably that first instant when I stumbled into him at the hospital, and looked up into his eyes. I felt I could see a whole future there, stretching right into eternity.

With every week that passed, Jonathan and I grew more inseparable. His interest in my work was genuine, and I found myself sketching shopping malls and office complexes to go with his landscape designs.

Six months into our courtship, we were walking through a misty fog in San Francisco, through Washington Square, when Jonathan stopped and turned to me. "I think I'm falling in love with you, Heather," he whispered. "No. I know I am."

Gulp. What do I say?

"Don't say anything," he whispered, reading my mind as he pulled me close. "Just think about it for the next few months, and let's see if this is going to be, you know, it."

We pulled apart, and I'm sure my face gave me away. "Okay," I said. "I'll pretend I have no idea whether I want to spend the rest of my life with the most amazing man I've ever met. You let me know when to reveal what I already think."

He grinned, and kissed me again. "Deal."

\* \* \*

Two days later I met with the girls for lunch.

"So did he propose or not?" Tanya asked.

"I don't know!" I said. "I guess not. I mean, he didn't say exact words or anything. I think he's just, kind of, preparing me for later or something."

"You always tip your hand," Ships scolded. "You never should have let the Spauldings tell him how you felt when you first met. That gave him all the power in the relationship."

I laughed. "All the power? You're crazy. And . . ." I nodded toward Crystal. "I did try to get them not to tell."

"Hey, don't look at me," Crystal said. "I was having Christian at the time."

"You have to, you know, do a dance," Ships went on. "Play hard to get at least a little bit."

"I can't do it," I said. "My face gives me away. I'm just a horrible liar."

Crystal nodded. "Me too. I can't pretend I'm not in love. It just shows."

"Well, I'd ask him to fish or cut bait," Tanya said. "Does he want to marry you or not?"

"Why push it?" I said. "We've only known each other six months. I'd feel a lot better if we had at least a year or two behind us."

Tanya shook her head. "But you know he's the one."

I smiled dreamily. "Yeah . . ."

"And you want to have children with him?" Ships asked.

"Oh, yeah," I said, without even thinking. Then I realized that, for the first time the concept didn't scare me to death.

"See?" Crystal said. "When you finally fall in love . . ."

I looked at them, from one to the other. "It's true! You guys were right!"

They all nodded, mumbling about having told me so, and playing the wise elders.

"I just hope you tie the knot after I have the baby," Tanya said. "I want to be back in my size eights before you squeeze me into a bridesmaid dress." Tanya patted her barely pregnant tummy. "And this had better not be twins."

"Got it," I said. "Oh—and you'll have to let me know about auditions, because I *sure* want to plan around those!"

"And the right time of the month," Ships reminded me.

I sighed. "Maybe I'll let you guys plan the whole thing," I joked.

They all gasped with delight and sat up straight, eager to take over.

"I'm kidding, I'm kidding," I said. "Sheesh. Talk about power fiends."

"But don't you at least want our ideas?" Ships asked.

"No."

"How about if we just help with the invitations and the center-pieces?" Crystal asked.

"No."

"Oh, come on," Tanya said. "You know we wouldn't let you down. Let us do your wedding."

"Hey. I don't even have a proposal yet, you guys." I laughed and twirled my lemonade.

"Well, my folks could probably arrange that, too," Crystal laughed.

"No, no, no," I said. "Please. I love you guys, but let's just let this one happen naturally."

They scowled but finally acquiesced. "Okay, then, we'll just give you a list of things *not* to do," Ships said cheerily.

They all pulled out their pens.

"Fine, fine, if it will keep you occupied," I said. "Tanya, are you going to eat that muffin?"

"No, and neither are you," she said. "You can't get fat for your wedding."

Crystal laughed. "I don't think you have to worry about Olive Oyl here getting fat. When she's finally pregnant, she'll probably look like a string with a knot in it."

"Maybe I should try to plump up," I said, reaching for Tanya's muffin.

She pulled it away, then reconsidered and handed it over. "Maybe it will go to your bustline," she whispered, wiggling her eyebrows.

"Gee, thanks," I said. "Guess I need all the help I can get."

"If it works, let me know," Crystal laughed.

* * *

As the months passed, Jonathan and I continued dating. I finally landed a design account, for a catalogue that sold upscale children's wear. It wasn't high fashion, but it was what I had trained for, and the people I worked with were fabulous. It was a career I could do from home, and it still left me time to work with Janice on window treatments. There was no time left for fashion photography, however. But I hadn't enjoyed that much, anyway. I kept thinking of artsy photos to take, instead of commercial ones. When one day I developed a whole roll of various shots of wet pebbles, I realized textures and colors were more exciting to me than teenagers' faces.

Jonathan was thrilled for me, finally having my own line of clothes. And I had a growing clientele of socialites in the area who occasionally asked me to design something just for them. One was even quoted in the newspaper as saying my dresses "always seem to be in motion—there's an energy in her lines." Jonathan said that reminded him of the blue dress I had worn to the art exhibit. "I noticed the same thing. You'd be standing still, but you'd look like you were swirling. Or maybe I was just swooning."

"It was just a bias cut." I shrugged.

Jonathan shrugged. "All gifted people think that what they do is no big deal, that anyone else could do it if they tried."

Actually I *had* thought that from time to time.

He kissed me on the forehead. "In that dress you looked like some kind of ethereal . . . fairy or a sprite or something . . . you were simply magical."

*Okay, I'll marry you.*

"Why do your clothes always look like they're swirling?" Jonathan asked.

And then I remembered. The day I was baptized, the water and light kept swirling around me and I felt lifted up to heaven. That same feeling came over me whenever I was sketching, creating ideas. I thought about Heavenly Father, how He created the world, and wondered if He had a similar rush of excitement with every new idea.

"Do you ever think about how we met?" Jonathan asked. "About that . . . you know, confusion?"

I cringed. *Every minute of every day.* "Not that much," I said. "You?"

"Nah. It's just funny now." He pulled me close.

*Yeah, right. Funny.*

Jonathan's business was doing great, as well. He'd hired on four new people, just since I'd met him, to handle various facets of the work. He had also just signed a huge shopping center client that would probably double his income this year.

\* \* \*

"No reason not to propose," Tanya said at our next gathering, taking only one bite of apple pie before pushing the plate away.

"We'll see." I couldn't help beaming at the idea.

"You have to let us know the minute it happens," Ships said, stealing a bite of Tanya's pie.

"You know, pie is supposed to be one of the worst things you can eat," I said. "I read a list somewhere about fat content. Let's see . . . chicken pot pie, cinnamon rolls, French-dipped beef sandwiches, croissants—"

"I'll bet French fries are on there," Crystal said. "And donuts."

"Yep," I said. "And gravies and sauces. Custards, too."

Tanya frowned. "You have just listed all my favorite foods."

"Well, I don't care," Ships said, helping herself to another bite of pie. "I'm married to an Italian, and they like their women with meat on them."

"Yeah, but not with pie dough on them," Tanya pointed out.

* * *

That weekend we all went, as couples, to see Tanya in a play. She'd been debating about whether to invite us, because, as she whispered to us girls, she was really playing herself. We weren't supposed to tell the guys this, because she didn't want Preston to know.

In her other plays, she'd played parts like a nosy landlady, a frightened college girl, an insane grandmother, and a murderous peasant woman. This time, she said, she was able to draw directly on her own feelings. And the director actually liked that she was pregnant for the role; he thought that added yet another dimension.

We settled into our seats and prepared for a delightful evening.

Instead, Crystal, Ships, and I found ourselves in shock. Tanya was playing a miserable young wife, whose relationship with her husband was falling apart. It was even sadder because she was pregnant.

During intermission, we went out to the lobby, a gold-gilded, Baroque-ish room with red velvet swags on the sides and spongy crimson carpet under our feet. The guys were all standing there with their 7-Ups, talking about what great talent she has, how gripping the story was, how you could sympathize with both characters, and how exhausting all the roles must be.

We girls huddled in a corner behind a velvet swag, and whispered in panic, "*This* is Tanya?" "Is she trying to tell us her marriage is on the rocks?" "Does Preston know?" "Can this be true?"

As we went back in for the second act, Jonathan rubbed my shoulders. "Hey, you guys look so worried—it's only acting, Heather. Don't take it to heart."

I gulped, but didn't say anything.

"What did you do when she stabbed that fisherman in her last play? Call the police?" he chuckled.

I forced a weak smile and the curtain went up. What if she killed the husband?

Thankfully, the play ended with a reconciliation, and the main characters resolving to work out their differences. It wasn't a happy ending, though, because neither one seemed sincerely healed. If anything, it was depressing.

Crystal and Ships felt the same way, as we dragged out of the theatre and made excuses to go on home without stopping for ice cream.

The next morning my phone rang. Ships was calling an emergency luncheon. We all gathered in a booth at a noisy deli where no one would hear our conversation. As Tanya walked in, we all stood and gave her a huge group hug.

"Was that character really you, hon?" Crystal asked, hesitantly.

Tanya nodded and sat down. "I am so miserable," she said, her voice cracking and the tears welling.

"We had no idea!" Ships said. "Why didn't you tell us?"

Tanya shook her head. "I don't know. I keep trying to work things out. But Preston is just . . . *not there.*"

"What—he doesn't come home at nights?" I asked.

"No, he's there, but he's just . . . this vacant, uninvolved person. He has no personality. None. He's just a lump."

Crystal frowned. "Tanya, you might just be going through the post-honeymoon thing, that's all. You see his faults, you've fallen into a routine, the excitement has worn off. You'll get over this."

We all chimed in our agreement.

Tanya shook her head. "No, I don't think so. I don't think he's ever going to change."

I wanted to ask why she had married him, then, but I didn't dare. She answered my question anyway.

"I married him because he was so supportive of my acting," she sniffled. "I thought supportive was a good thing."

"It is," Ships said. "So what happened?"

"It's like he doesn't care," Tanya said. "If I'm going to be late, that's fine. If I need to get away from the house to work on my lines, that's fine. It's like he's a robot. There's no emotion."

"But . . ." I frantically searched for something positive in the situation, "he does give you the freedom you wanted."

"I know," Tanya said. "But I want passion. I want excitement. He's just dull."

"Uh-oh," Crystal said. "I saw this on a talk show. It was called 'Wild Women and Mild Men.' They interviewed all these high-strung women—not that you're high-strung, Tanya, but you know. Anyway, they had all picked these quiet husbands because they offered stability and calm. And the men liked that the women were these bundles of energy all the time."

"And?" Ships asked.

"And then they each started to resent the other one," Crystal said. "The women said the husbands were boring, and the husbands said their wives were wearing them out and being too flighty. Not that you're flighty, Tanya."

"Well, that certainly describes Preston and me," she said. "Remember when I told you guys I was waiting for fireworks? I guess I should have kept waiting."

We all sat silently for a moment.

"So what are you going to do?" Ships finally asked.

Tanya released a big sigh. "Nothing."

"Nothing?" I asked.

"It can't be fixed," Tanya said. "You'll find this out once you get married, Heather. Some things can be fixed, and some can't.

There's a basic nature to Preston, and this is it. He can't become someone else. And I can't tone down, either. We're stuck."

Crystal patted Tanya on the back. "I'm glad you're not thinking of getting a divorce," she said, glancing meaningfully at Tanya's pregnant stomach.

"Oh, I know," Tanya said. "I have the baby to think about. So I'm going to stay, and we'll manage somehow. It's just not . . . what I always dreamed of."

"I don't feel like eating," Ships said. "You guys?"

"Nah," I said. "Let's just get some sodas and talk."

We tried to buoy up Tanya's feelings, but we couldn't seem to break through her hopelessness.

"Well, I say you quit the play, then," Ships said. "I mean, you're really good in it and all, but it just reminds you every day how unhappy you are. I mean, you can never escape it."

Tanya shrugged. "That's true. Maybe I'll feel better when I go back to playing killer peasants."

"There you go," I said. "Don't take roles that bring you down. Stick with crazed villains or something."

Tanya smiled. "Good idea. *Those* parts don't remind me of my marriage."

"There. See?" Crystal sounded relieved. "At least you don't want to kill him."

We all laughed, even Tanya. I lifted my 7-Up in a toast, and said, "There's always something to celebrate."

# Piña Colada Shake

1 cup vanilla ice cream
3/4 cup pineapple juice
1/4 cup cream of coconut
whipped cream

This is the perfect splurge drink to make, when you want something rich, yet refreshing. And it's so easy that we girls make it whenever we find ourselves gathered together in one of our kitchens.

In a blender, whirl ice cream, pineapple juice, and cream of coconut until smooth. Pour into a frosty glass and top with whipped cream.

Serves 1.

# Chapter 6

*Let thy soul delight in thy husband . . .*
D&C 25:14

The first time I saw Maxine, she was on the news. "Anytime you want to get something done," she said, "just ask the Mormons. The Mormon *women.*"

I busted up laughing and turned up the sound. She was an impeccably dressed, diamond-ring-waving woman with chic gray hair, loading boxes into the back of a van.

A reporter was asking her about a food drive, and Maxine was ticking off the labels of various boxes, explaining how these canned goods would be utilized by a local soup kitchen.

"We run the show," she said, winking at the reporter as if no one else could hear her.

*That woman is a hoot. I wonder if the Church knows she's running around saying things like that.* It seemed like good publicity for the humanitarian work we do, so I was pleased to see the story getting covered.

Then, a month later, she showed up in my home ward. I knew I had to meet her, and the minute I did, we clicked. We chattered all the way to Gospel Doctrine class, then again on the way to Relief Society, and then out into the parking lot. Widowed a year earlier, she had decided to scale down from her large house in San Mateo, and moved into our ward boundaries. She had been a stake Relief Society president, and was now working at the Oakland Temple.

She was thirty-five years older than I was, older than my own mom, but we became instant girlfriends. We were soon lunch buddies as well. "You have to meet my group," I said. "They will adore you."

So I brought her to the next luncheon, and of course the other girls felt the same way about her. She wasn't exactly a mother figure, but she was lovably spunky, and had the wonderful advantage of having already gone through the things we were worrying about, so she could always put things into perspective for us again.

We invited her to our next luncheon, and our next, and before we knew it, Maxine was a permanent fixture in our group; a woman we felt we had known all our lives. It was Maxine who told us what a waste of time it was to fret so much over potty-training, or whether kids are getting all the food groups in every meal. She taught us to trust our own instincts, to dare to be the unpopular mother, to teach kids work habits early, and to make our husbands feel like heroes. She lived what she preached, and soon we were all following her example, and getting up half an hour early every day (well, most days) to read scriptures. When we went out as couples, we always invited Maxine, and the guys adored her as well.

Jonathan loved the stories she would tell about her late husband, Sam—a man with flaws, to be certain, but a giant in the eyes of his wife. Maxine told it like it was: if they'd had an argument, then it was a doozy. But she always remembered their promises in the temple, and knew they could make the marriage work, if both of them had the commitment.

"I am so glad you found Maxine," Crystal whispered several weeks after the first luncheon she attended. "Maybe she can help Tanya with her marriage."

I had been praying for the same thing, and squeezed Crystal's hand. Tanya's baby was due in another month, and we were all hoping her spirits would lift after having the baby. Crystal attested to the "entirely different person" you become when you're pregnant, so we were banking on Tanya's pendulum swinging back toward the middle again.

One night after Jonathan and I had dinner at Maxine's, including her famous "berry good" crumb pie, we were taking a shortcut through the city, when I glanced over and noticed he was crying.

I brushed the tear from his cheek. "What is it?" I asked gently.

Jonathan pulled over and stopped the car. "That woman," he said, nodding back toward Maxine's place, "is the answer to my prayers."

I raised my eyebrows. "Uh . . . okay."

He smiled and pulled me to him. "I've wanted to ask you for . . . well, since our first date, really."

*Ask me? Ask me what?*

"But I kept thinking I had to be perfect for you. I just couldn't believe that you'd want to marry someone with all my faults . . ."

*Marry? Did I hear the word* marry?

"I know I don't deserve you," Jonathan went on, "but when I hear her talk about how much she loved Sam, and yet all her stories are about how he wasn't perfect, well, I thought . . ." He took a breath. "If you'll be my Maxine, I'll try to be your Sam."

"Are you serious?" Okay, I know it was a crazy question, given that this crying man looked about as serious as a man can possibly look. But I just couldn't believe my ears. Maybe I needed to hear it again.

"Will you marry me, Heather?" Jonathan held my hands in his now, and kissed them.

I threw my arms around him. "Oh, yes. Yes, I'll marry you. I love you, Jonathan." We hugged, we kissed, and we held each other again. We wiped each other's tears, we laughed, and we cried some more. It was at least twenty minutes before either of us looked outside and realized he had parked in front of a bail bonds shop.

"Uh . . . could you propose to me again in another location?" I asked. "This one doesn't make the best, uh, story to tell our kids . . ."

Jonathan was laughing. "And we already have one funny story," he said.

*Exactly.*

So Jonathan started the car and pulled up Chestnut Street, where the lights of San Francisco twinkled across the bay, and moonlight danced on the leaves of the magnolia trees. We stepped out of the car, and Jonathan leaned me back against the door. "Will you be my bride?" he breathed into my ear.

"Oh, yeah," I said. "And believe me, you are plenty perfect."

He smiled, and traced my cheek with one finger. "Plenty perfect. I like that."

We drove to my parents' house and I ran up the steps. "Wake up," I called, as I burst through the front door. "It's Heather and Jonathan!"

My parents were in the family room watching television, but came running out looking alarmed. "What? What?"

"We're engaged!" I shouted.

My mother pressed her hands against her heart and began to cry. Dad gave Jonathan a bear hug.

"Oh, wait—shouldn't you have asked permission?" I turned to Jonathan.

"He already had it." Dad was waving away my concern. "I told him months ago that if he ever wanted to join this family, he'd be a welcome addition."

"Dad!"

"What?"

"That is so embarrassing. You brought it up first?"

Dad shrugged. "Hey, you're not getting any younger, Sweet Pea."

I gasped. "If I weren't so happy right now, I'd be furious with you," I said, slapping at his arm. Then I turned to Mom. "Can you believe he did that?"

"It was okay with me," she said. Jonathan gave her a hug.

"So you were all three in on this?" I couldn't believe it.

"I was just waiting for the right time," Jonathan said.

I got right in his face and mouthed the words, "Bail bonds?" and he laughed.

"Well, let's forget about all that," Mom said (such a Mom line), "and let's talk about the wedding."

So we chose a date five months away (yes, I remembered to calculate), and a reception hall.

"Tomorrow we can lock in the reservation," Mom said. "Then you'll need to choose a photographer, a caterer, a florist, invitations . . ." Mom had obviously been putting more thought into this than she would admit. "I'll bet Heather already has her dress designed," she said.

I swallowed. "Not really," I said. "I think I was afraid I'd jinx it, so I didn't want to plan it out until it was definite."

"Well, start sketching, baby," Jonathan said as he headed into the kitchen. "Because, ready or not, I am marrying you." He was opening the fridge now, and pouring himself a glass of orange juice.

I watched him, smiling. When I glanced at Mom and Dad, they had the same dreamy expressions on their faces as they watched Jonathan make himself at home.

"It doesn't get better than this," Dad whispered.

I was thinking the same thing, but then Mom whispered back, "Oh, yes, it does—grandkids!"

* * *

I was still beaming the next morning when I called the girls and announced an emergency luncheon. They were all anticipating news of the engagement, and bustled into Scoma's at the wharf like it was Free Shrimp Day.

"Quick! We need a table," Tanya said. The hostess seemed taken aback, and glanced down at Tanya's belly, then over at me.

"Not for a delivery," I laughed. But she showed us to a booth near a door, just in case.

"Okay," I said, as we settled into our seats. All the girls leaned in. "He asked me!"

A scream rose up from our table, and other diners glanced over. The girls were cheering and high-fiving each other, and Maxine teared up.

"Did someone just find out they're having a baby?" the waiter asked, looking at Tanya's pregnant belly.

"Yeah, right," she deadpanned. "I just found out two minutes ago. What we're celebrating is an engagement!"

"And not a moment too soon," I added, patting Tanya on the back.

"Not me!" she shrieked indignantly. "Her!"

Now all the customers were applauding and I could feel my face reddening.

Eventually the commotion died down and I was able to give the girls a detailed account (excluding the bail bonds shop, of course).

Maxine was crying in earnest now. "I feel so honored to have been mentioned in a proposal," she said.

"But you should never have told him he was perfect," Ships said. "You tipped your hand again."

"That's right," Tanya said. "Now he'll never make any changes for you."

"I don't want a single change," I said. "He is beyond wonderful."

Crystal smiled. "You'll want to change him," she said. "Every woman does."

"That's true," Maxine said, "but we shouldn't. Men really don't like it," she pointed out.

We all laughed at the craziness of women trying to change their men, and the men resisting it all the way.

"What would you change about Peter?" I asked Crystal.

"Oh, his family. I'd give him another set of parents. Or at least a new mother."

"I'd change Preston's entire personality," Tanya mumbled.

"I'd change Marco's driving—he makes me crazy how he screeches around turns," Ships said. "He drives like a parking valet."

"Oh, you could all make your lists," Maxine said. "Goodness knows I made mine, but you could make an even longer list of the things you hope will *never* change. Just remember that, ladies. Be grateful for the good men you have. Don't get caught up in all that complaining wives do."

"Maxine is right," Crystal said. "We are all very blessed. Well, except Tanya."

Tanya smirked as we all cracked up, then said, "Hey. He doesn't eat much, doesn't wet the bed, and doesn't borrow my shampoo—I guess that's my list."

We were all laughing now, and hugging Tanya. "That's not such a bad list. If anybody can make it work, you can," I said. The girls all agreed.

"I wish I could light a firecracker in that man's pants," Maxine said, as if thoughtfully studying the best way to fix Tanya's marital woes.

We all laughed again, and Tanya muttered, "Don't think I haven't thought about it . . ."

We ordered our seafood, and then I asked, "So how come men don't try to change their wives as much as wives try to change their husbands?"

Ships spat an ice cube back into her water. "Oh, I can tell you that. Men don't notice our faults. All they really want is a hot meal and—"

I screamed to interrupt her before she could say something embarrassing again. "Okay, I'm sorry I asked," I said.

Crystal was giggling. "Really, men are not complex creatures. When you think about it, their needs are very simple. And unless you're really at one end of the bell curve, they don't notice that anything's wrong."

"Oh, come on," I said. "These are not apes we're talking about."

Tanya laughed. "Apes would be more complex."

"They would not," I said, but I laughed. "Men want certain things, too."

"Like I said," Ships started in again, "a hot meal—"

"No, it's true," Maxine said. "They don't talk about it as much as we do, but I think most men do notice things, and appreciate it when they have good wives."

"And if the wives aren't so good?" I asked.

"They still won't say much," Maxine said. "Mostly they stay pretty quiet. But they do get sad."

We all just sat there for a moment, taking in the—well, *sadness* of what Maxine had just said.

"How awful," I finally said. "To just live out your marriage in quiet sadness."

"I say it's their own fault if they can't learn to speak up," Ships said. "Who wants a taste of this Cioppino? It's excellent."

Maxine took a sip. "And there's another difference right there. A man would enjoy it, but do you know any man who would offer a sip to the other men at his table?"

"What if Jonathan wishes I'd change, but just never says so?" I said, almost to myself.

"Then count your lucky stars," Tanya said. "You don't have to do it."

"Heather, you're not even married to him yet." Crystal took a bite of her sourdough bread. "Don't worry. He'll be thrilled speechless."

I sighed. "Yeah, I'm sure that's it."

"Oh, stop worrying," Ships said. "You guys will have a great marriage. You're perfect for each other. We all think so."

* * *

The next day Jonathan took me ring shopping. "I knew you better than to pick something myself," Jonathan smiled. "I am marrying a woman of definite tastes and opinions."

I spotted a solitaire in a swirly setting on the way in, but tried on several others just to seem less impulsive. Finally I pulled Jonathan back to the front case, and pointed it out.

"Wow," he said. "That looks like something you'd design yourself. Let's get it. Only let's make the stone a little larger."

I have to admit, my eyes danced. Yes, I'd love to tell you I couldn't care less what size stone is on my eternal wedding band. But the second he said that, I wanted to squeal, "Yes! Yes! Bigger!"

When we went to pick it up, and he slid it onto my finger, it was even more dazzling than I had remembered.

"You look radiant," Jonathan said.

"I *feel* radiant," I said. "Like I'm wearing a miniature temple on my hand."

Jonathan kissed me. "That's exactly what I was thinking."

The wedding band was a perfect complement to the single stone, and we picked out a masculine version of the same band for Jonathan.

The next five months were a blur of wedding arrangements. Besides the usual bridal details, LDS couples have temple arrangements to make, clothes to buy for the temple ceremony, and interviews to complete.

"Well, it's a joy to give you this," the stake president said as he signed my temple recommend and slid it across the table to me. "I hope you two will settle in our stake, so we won't be losing you."

"Oh, we are," I said. "We've bought a house. Jonathan and I have both been saving up, and we're going to be in the Second Ward." As I stood up to leave, I pulled a photo out of my purse and showed him the little house we had picked.

"Sit down again," President Bickmore said. "I want to show you something."

He took out his own wallet, then reached in and took out a small, worn photo and handed it to me. "That was our first home," he said. "It's where we raised our children. And that's where I hope to live in the life to come—or in one just like it."

I looked at the aging photo. A trim little clapboard house with a neat front porch sat a few feet back from the sidewalk. A young couple posed proudly on the steps. It was quite a different house than the sprawling estate where I knew he lived today.

"That's me and my bride," he said. "I carry that everywhere I go."

When I looked up and saw tears in his eyes, I, too, began to cry. We just sat there, trying to control our breathing and our tear ducts, releasing sudden laughs, and then crying again.

"Well," he said, taking a big breath and rising to his feet, "real estate does that to you."

I laughed; President Bickmore was a realtor.

"Whenever we sing about the Lord preparing mansions for us, it's that humble little house I picture," he added.

I sniffled. "Because of the love in it," I said.

He shook my hand. "Because of the love in it."

# "Berry Good" Crumb Pie

1 cup crushed pecans
2 cups flour
1 cup sugar, divided
3/4 cup butter
1 1/2 Tablespoons cornstarch
1 cup raspberries
1 cup blueberries or sliced strawberries

I had to pry this recipe away from Maxine. She had told me it was quite difficult to make, so I'd be more impressed. Maxine likes to exaggerate, let's say. But now she would have to admit that it is a snap to throw together.

In a large bowl, mix pecans, flour, and half the sugar. Cut butter into flour mixture with a pastry blender or two knives, until it forms pea-sized crumbs. Press half of this mixture into the bottom and sides of a pie plate.

In a medium bowl, mix remaining half of sugar and cornstarch. Fold in berries. Spoon mixture into crust, then top with remaining flour mixture. Bake at 350 degrees for 30 minutes. Serve warm.

Makes 6 servings.

# Chapter 7

*A woman when she is in travail hath sorrow, because her hour is come: but as soon as she is delivered of the child, she remembereth no more the anguish, for joy that a man is born into the world.*

John 16:21

"Why on earth would you want this experience?" Tanya teased Ships, when we came to see her and the new baby at the hospital.

We all laughed, as Tanya told us about "the worst labor" and "the worst delivery" in the history of womankind. Crystal just chuckled, shaking her head.

"I'm telling you," Tanya said, looking at Ships. "Do not pass go. Do not collect two hundred dollars." Then she whipped around to give me the same advice. "You either."

"Oh, come on," I chided her. "If it were that bad, nobody would do it more than one time."

"And I'm not," Tanya said. "This is it. Preston can take on another wife if he wants to; I don't care."

"You'll change your mind," Crystal said. "Trust me."

"Well, at least it's a joyous occasion," I deadpanned. "Where everyone's so happy about a new little bundle coming to earth."

Tanya smirked. "And I can't even tell you how much *fun* nursing is."

"Oh, enough complaining," Maxine said. "Let's see the little doll!"

Tanya asked for her baby, and soon a nurse brought in a squealing little thing with a red face and dark, fuzzy hair.

"Hey, look," Ships said. "She's exactly like her mom!"

Tanya nuzzled little Molly, who started to quiet down. "These are your aunties," she said. "Don't listen to anything they tell you."

We stood there, marveling at the tiny hands, the darling feet, the wee lips. And I realized, I really did want to be Molly's aunt. I loved her, suddenly, and felt a pledge welling in my heart, to help her get home again to her Heavenly Father. Something impressed upon my heart that He missed her already, and loved her unspeakably. *Oh, Molly, pray to Him often; let Him know you remember.*

"What are you crying for?" Tanya said.

I hadn't even realized I was crying. "She is just . . . so . . . precious," I said.

Tanya grinned and squeezed my hand. "Don't cry, or you'll get me started."

I looked at Crystal and Ships, who were also tearing up.

"Oh, great—a whole blubbering group," Tanya said, wiping her eyes. "You'll have to be the one to hold it together," she said to Maxine.

"That's right," Maxine said. "After all, I'm the driver."

There were only a few months between Molly's birth and my wedding. I invited all the girls over for a "Mormon tea," to show them the bridesmaid dress designs. I poured grenadine juice into the teacups, then served scones with crème fraîche. Tanya was grousing that she didn't have enough time to lose weight, until she saw how slimming the dresses were that I had designed for them. Each one was different, but all of them were a shimmering coral-peach shade, the darling color of the seventies. Tanya's had a tunic, which nicely hid her "fluffy middle," as we decided to call it. Ships's dress had a dramatic Jean Harlow neckline, Crystal's crisscrossed at her tiny waist, making her look (almost) voluptuous, and Maxine's had a floor-length jacket Grace Kelly would have envied.

As for my own dress, I designed a simple yet elegant gown. It swept to the floor in a hush of white fabric, like delicate icing drizzled over a sweet confection. Scattered glass beading guided the eye up to a high, lacy neckline that Jonathan said made me look like a blond Audrey Hepburn. I felt like an absolute princess.

* * *

Jonathan filled the reception hall with ferns and flowers until it looked like a lush grotto in Hawaii, somewhere only your fantasies could take you.

The caterer got sick, the photographer went ballistic when his camera battery died, and two guests got into a heated dispute over a parking space. But none of it mattered, because that same morning, we had been sealed for time and eternity in the most glorious sealing room I had ever seen. Granted, it was the only one I had ever seen, but it took my breath away, and made me wonder if we had stepped, for a moment, through the veil and into heaven. My parents were crying. Jonathan's parents were crying. In fact, everyone but the sealer was crying, and after the ceremony, no one wanted to leave. We all just wanted to stay and bask in the beautiful, sacred feeling of the temple.

So, when every last detail of the reception didn't come together perfectly, we couldn't have cared less. I danced to "The Way You Look Tonight" with my father, kissed my mother and told her I wanted to be just like her, cut the cake, and then scooted out of the reception hall with Jonathan, amidst fluttering white feathers instead of rice. I had married the man of my dreams and I couldn't imagine feeling anything but blissful joy.

Two glorious weeks in the San Juan Islands followed, and when we came back we opened wedding presents (including seven Crock-Pots and five fondue sets, all avocado green). I twirled through the rooms of our new house, pushed bookcases, plants, and sofas around until I liked the arrangement, and placed all our shoes on racks. I lined up our kitchen canisters, studied the oven manual, stacked dishes, and carefully placed every knife, fork, and spoon in the appropriate compartments.

I was just nailing our new window valance boxes into place, when Tanya called. "Okay, enough nesting," she said. (Did she know me or what?) "Time for another lunch."

I arrived early, and was glad to see Ships and Tanya had already settled in. Ships's kids were in school, but Tanya had brought little

Molly along in a carrier with a pink hood, folded back now to show the little sleeping princess.

"She's grown!" I gasped.

"Babies do that," Tanya said. "They change so much even in one week."

"Well, that's the last time I leave for a two-week honeymoon, then!"

"How come Crystal's boys didn't seem to grow that fast?" Ships asked.

Tanya shrugged. "Crystal and Peter are small people. Their kids will probably wear the actual sizes of their ages for twenty years! Molly's already off the chart. She wears 2-T."

Off the chart. 2-T. Here were two expressions I'd never heard, but which would become part of our vocabulary now.

"I guess Gino and Francesca will be small, too," Ships said. "Marco's only five-nine."

"But you're tall," I said, stupidly.

Tanya and Ships just stared at me.

"Oh, yeah," I laughed. "I keep forgetting. I mean, they're yours, and I forget that they're stepchildren."

Ships pursed her lips. "They may be the only kids I'll ever have."

"Oh, come on, now," Tanya said. "I'm the drama queen, remember? You can't give up yet. You'll get pregnant."

"We're seeing a fertility specialist," Ships whispered. "And it doesn't look very promising."

"Oh," I said, reaching for her hand. "They can do amazing things these days. I keep reading about miracle pregnancies—"

"I know," Ships said, "but it doesn't always work. We've tried so many things already. Prayers, blessings . . . our love life is so scheduled now, it's awful—everything goes by the calendar and by my temperature. You can't imagine how unromantic it is to make it all so mechanical."

Tanya frowned and hugged her. "You poor thing."

"My heart breaks every time I see a pregnant woman. And I've stopped going to baby showers completely," she admitted.

I wanted to tell her she could always adopt. Or to just relax, because that's when so many women finally get pregnant. Or that she was lucky to have two already. But I sensed every one of those comments would be the wrong thing to say.

"I wish I knew what I could do," I said. "It must be so hard for you, Ships."

She sighed, fanning away the tears welling in her eyes. "Just knowing you guys are there helps," she said. "I know I can share this with you, and you won't tell me to just relax or some stupid thing."

I gulped.

"It's like I'm grieving a loss," Ships said. "I've wanted to have babies all my life, and now—" She snapped her fingers. "The dream is gone."

Tanya hugged her tighter. "Are you sure? I hate to hear you sound so—so final."

"It's useless," Ships said, her voice cracking. We've been trying since day one."

"And you're such a wonderful mom," I said. "It isn't fair."

"Gino and Francesca are really lucky kids," Tanya agreed.

Ships forced a smile. "Thanks, you guys. I am grateful for them. I just—well, you know how I feel."

I leaned my head on her shoulder. "It's so hard to understand why life goes the way it does at times."

Ships nodded. "It sure is."

None of us had noticed Crystal dashing in, but suddenly she appeared at our table with Christian and Andrew in her arms. A waitress helped her strap Christian into his chair, and as she plopped little Andrew onto the booth seat, she looked up and blurted, "Guess what, you guys?—I'm pregnant again!"

Ships caught her breath, and then burst into tears.

"What? Did I say the wrong thing?" Cystal asked.

Tanya moved so Ships could scoot out and dash to the ladies' room. "I'll be right back," Ships whispered, pushing past a confused waitress.

"We'll need a few more minutes," I smiled at the waitress.

"What happened?" Crystal asked.

So we told her. Crystal withered as she realized how her happy news must have struck Ships. "I need to go apologize—" she said, starting to get up.

"Just wait here," Tanya said, pulling her back down again. "You know Ships. She'll want to cry by herself."

We all waited, morosely wondering what we could say or do to ease the situation. When Ships came back, her face was splashed clean, but her eyes were still red.

"Oh, honey, I love you," Crystal said, jumping up to hug her. "I would never say anything to hurt—"

"I know," Ships said, scooting in next to me. "You didn't know. It's not your fault. I just need to get a grip on this." She waved away our back patting and said, "I didn't mean to take away from your announcement, either."

"Oh, forget the announcement," Crystal said. "What's important right now is you. What can we do to help you?"

"Just cry with me," Ships said, new tears shining in her eyes.

At that moment Maxine finally arrived, shopping bags and a huge purse under her arms. "Good gracious," she said, "with all these babies there's no room for *stuff*."

Then she noticed the somber mood at the table, and said, "Did somebody die?"

Ships chuckled through her tears, and we all scooted around the booth to make room for Maxine.

"I can't have any babies," Ships whispered. Then she burst into tears again, apologizing through her napkin.

"Neither can I!" Maxine nearly shouted, as if thrilled to be finding something in common.

"Yes, but you're . . ."

"Too old? Heavens, yes," Maxine laughed. "But that's not what I mean. Honey, I'm sterile as a stick. Sam and I were never able to have children. Why do you think I've glommed onto this sad little group?"

Tanya elbowed her and laughed.

"I thank my lucky stars," Maxine said, "that I'll be able to have children in the next life, when Satan will be bound, and it will be a whole lot easier."

"So you just . . . accepted it? That easily?" Ships asked.

"Oh, not at first," Maxine said. "Of course I cried. You need to cry. Crying brings you to your knees so you can pray."

I smiled. Maxine always seemed so wise.

"But when you pray, and you can honestly say, 'Thy will be done,' then you'll be okay. You have to listen. God had other plans for me, and He probably has other plans for you."

"But what about *my* plans?" Ships asked.

"You'll just have to make God's plans your plans," Maxine said. "That's the whole purpose of prayer, if you ask me."

We all sat for a moment, taking that in. She had pegged it, in a nutshell. Instead of deciding what we wanted and then begging for it, we needed to learn God's will. Of course, that takes humility and patience, two traits we were all short on.

Ships's chin was still quivering. "I'm not ready to let go of my dream, Maxine."

Maxine smiled and reached across the table for Ships's hand. "I know, dear. But let me give you something else to consider. If Heavenly Father knows your deepest desires, which He does . . ." and she looked at us for nods and agreement, "then He knows how much you want to be a mother. Right?"

We all nodded.

"So, just maybe, he had a hand in your marriage to a man who had two children already."

Ships was crying again, but this time they were tears of gratitude. "He did that," she sniffled. "He did that for me, didn't He?"

"It doesn't matter whose body delivered those babies," Maxine said. "You're the one who shapes and molds them, and gets them back home to heaven. It's just as much the raising as the birthing that makes you a mother."

Ships released a huge sigh, and blew her nose. "I love you, Maxine," she said. "And I'm glad you didn't have any children, because if you did . . ." She wiped her nose again. "Then you might be out to lunch with them today, instead of me."

We all laughed, and Maxine squeezed her hand again.

"And I really needed you," Ships said.

Now we were all crying. I looked around the table at my dearest friends and realized that God's ways are so often unknown to us. Sometimes a missed opportunity paves the way for a better one taken later. And a childless woman can still be a mother, in the ways that matter most.

# Cranberry, Cheddar, & Almond Scones

Great for a fancy luncheon, but just as good for packing into a hiker's lunch. If you ever open a bed-and-breakfast, your guests will swoon over them.

2 cups buttermilk baking mix
1/4 cup butter, chilled and diced
1 cup sliced almonds, toasted
1 cup dried cranberries
1 cup cheddar cheese, shredded
1 cup lemon-flavored yogurt

In a large bowl, cut butter into baking mix until it forms pea-sized crumbs. Stir in remaining ingredients and scoop dollops onto a greased baking sheet. Bake at 425 degrees for 10 minutes, or until just beginning to turn golden. Remove from oven. And here's my secret for moist scones: Using a spatula, scoot scones together on baking sheet and cover with a clean towel. This retains their heat. Leave covered for 10 minutes, and they finish baking.

Serves 8.

# Creme Fraiche

1 cup cream
1 Tablespoon buttermilk

Place both in a lidded jar, and leave at room temperature for 24 hours. Mixture should thicken. Chill before serving.

Everyone seems to like different toppings for their scones. Maxine is a pure butter gal, Tanya likes marmalade, Ships goes for honey, and Crystal likes them plain. Try them any way you like.

# Chapter 8

*Seek ye out of the best books words of wisdom; seek learning, even by study and also by faith.*
D&C 88:118

Exactly eight months after that luncheon, two babies were delivered. One was Crystal's—her first girl—and one was mine and Jonathan's.

We couldn't get over how incredible it was that we both ended up in the hospital on the same day, and both had baby girls. Obviously I must have gotten pregnant on our honeymoon, and Crystal delivered early.

Jonathan wouldn't stop kissing me—my cheeks, my forehead, my hand—he was a fountain of emotion, and kept saying (too loudly, I told him) that ours was the prettiest baby in the whole hospital. He kept asking if I was comfortable, and finally I had to explain to him that the answer wouldn't be yes for about six more weeks, so he probably should stop asking.

It was adorable how attentive he was. He cut my steak into tiny pieces, wrapped my roll in a napkin and put it on the radiator to warm, and rubbed my feet as I ate dinner. If I had asked him to feed me, he probably would have done that, too.

"I love you so much," he said for the twentieth time that hour.

"Then stop making me laugh," I said, trying to stop again. "Laughing hurts the stitches."

"Oh no!" He looked like a claymation figure with two Cheerios for eyes. It only made me laugh harder. Watching him ooze this much love and devotion was honestly funny. It was as if he were doing a comedy act.

"Come and lie down next to me," I said, patting the bed.

Jonathan zoomed into place.

"You have to relax," I whispered, kissing him and stroking his hair.

"But it's so exciting," he whispered back, like a little kid with no better excuse.

I laughed again. "Yes, it's wonderful. It's exciting. We have a little daughter. You and me. And you were the best coach in the universe."

He smiled. "Okay, then."

I sighed. "Okay, then."

I heard a commotion in the hallway, and then the four grandparents burst into the room like a brass band, all talking at once.

"She's gorgeous!"

"Are you feeling okay?"

"Our first granddaughter!"

"There's the proud papa!"

"What a perfect baby!"

"Why are you in her bed, Jonathan?"

"That's right—that's how you got into this fix in the first place!"

Somehow I knew I'd better get used to laughing. And no sooner had they scooted out to the nursery window to get another look, than in barged Maxine, Tanya, and Ships.

"The aunties are here," Tanya sang. "We have everything under control."

"Yeah, right," I laughed. "You guys look like the three fairies in Sleeping Beauty."

"Oh, let's do that!" Maxine shouted. "We'll each grab a wand and bestow the little pumpkin with a gift."

They snatched up three drinking straws and went to wave them in front of the nursery window.

Soon the nurse brought the baby in, chuckling as she said, "I think the good fairies are watching over her." The girls followed her in, babbling away, and wearing crowns they had folded out of paper napkins from the lunch trays. They were still waving their wands.

"I gave her the gift of confidence," Tanya said, thrusting her chin out to show that she had plenty to spare.

"She's already beautiful, so I gave her brains." Maxine winked.

"And I gave her a 36-D bustline," Ships said.

"You what?" I almost sat up on my stitches. Jonathan's eyes bugged again.

"Hey, it's not immediate," Ships said defensively.

"Well, I certainly hope not!" Maxine laughed.

"It's the practical gift," Ships continued. "If she takes after Heather, she'll have nothing, so I figured—"

"You people," I muttered. "How does anyone get through this experience normally?"

Jonathan was just shaking his head in disbelief as Ships giggled and plopped down on the bed. "But you love us. How could you get through anything without us? I thought about giving her permanent eyeliner—"

Jonathan patted Ships on the back. "Such a thoughtful aunt."

The girls hardly listened. They were still buzzing with self-satisfaction, and then Tanya said, "Now we have to go give gifts to Crystal's baby."

*Poor Crystal.*

Finally Jonathan and I were alone. "It's so great to see Ships celebrating births, instead of resenting them," I said, stroking the fuzz on our baby's head.

"Yes." Jonathan agreed. "But she could celebrate with a little less focus on—"

"Oh, that's just Ships. Be glad she didn't bestow the gift of ten year's experience in precision marching."

Jonathan smiled and leaned down to our little bundle. "So, are we settled on her name?"

"Hayley Noelle," I said.

The next day, Crystal and I saw each other's babies, and hugged each other. "They can grow up together just like cousins," I said. "We'll even have double birthday parties!"

Crystal nodded. "Ashley and Hayley. They even sound like twins."

"So what did the Fairies give Ashley?" I remembered to ask.

Crystal smiled. "Let's see. Tanya gave her strength, so she can stand up to her big brothers."

"That's good; she'll need that."

"And Maxine gave her curiosity, so she'll learn everything in the world."

I nodded. "And Ships?"

Crystal shook her head. "Permanent eyeliner. Can you believe that?"

As Jonathan drove us home the next morning, I realized that what everyone had said was true: Nothing really prepares you for the level of pain you feel during labor. But nothing prepares you for the level of love you feel for that new little person, either. It's as if the doors to your heart have been unlocked and thrown wide for the first time.

While I was getting around reasonably well, I still needed lots of rest, and my mom was on hand to make sure I got it. That, and her homemade chicken soup. She ran pretty tight interference, only letting the girls visit at certain times of day. Eventually I figured out the best way for Hayley to nurse, and soon I was feeling back to my old self.

"Be sure to keep trying her clothes on her," Tanya advised. "Or she'll outgrow them before she can even wear them." This turned out to be true.

"Be sure to read to her," Ships said. "They develop language skills early." This, too, was good advice.

"Be sure to take lots of pictures," Maxine said. "I have to brag about *somebody's* babies." So we snapped away.

"I'm the one with the most kids and the least advice," Crystal said. "Honestly, I don't know what to tell anyone."

Crystal had had a much tougher time, since her two little boys still needed her attention as well. She told me over the phone that she'd never felt so exhausted. "Maybe I'm just not cut out for this."

*What? Where was the perpetually sunny Crystal?*

"I think we need an emergency luncheon," I said. Crystal agreed.

We met in Berkeley this time, at a great little bakery that also served soup and quiche. I placed Hayley's carrier next to me, where she gurgled and batted at the tiny mobile of stars hanging from the carrier handle.

"Nothing Italian," Ships sighed, closing her menu. "Oh well. France is close."

"Tell 'em to sprinkle some oregano into your soup," Maxine snapped. "You and that Italian food." Maxine was helping Molly drink apple juice from her bottle.

Ships smiled. "They're really the cuisine experts who taught the French, you know."

"Blah, blah, blah," Tanya said, still looking over the choices. "The cradle of culture, the land of Da Vinci, gateway to Europe . . ."

Now Ships was slapping her with the menu. "Well it *is*." She smiled. "At least you were listening."

"I'm having the butternut squash soup," Tanya said. "I love that."

"Me too," I said. "And that cheese bread they make."

Soon we had all ordered. Since I had called the luncheon, I leaned in and said, "Crystal, tell us what's going on."

Crystal smiled, took a big breath, then shrugged. "I'm just not happy."

Tanya stared at her. "That's it? You're not happy? For this I drove all the way to Berkeley? I wake up every day of my life and realize I'm not happy." Then she looked at me like I was a nut, to have called a meeting.

"Tanya," I said. "Does that sound like Crystal to you?"

Tanya cocked her head to one side, thinking. "No," she admitted. "Okay. What's up?"

"I don't know," Crystal said. "After having Ashley, I thought I'd just snap right back into being a mom, but—I feel detached or something. I can't seem to feel the joy I felt when I had the boys."

Maxine slapped her palm down on the table, making all of us jump. "It's baby blues!" she said. "You see it on talk shows all the time. Sometimes having a baby leaves you feeling blue, honey. That's all."

Ships grinned and slung one arm over Tanya's shoulders. "Of course, Tanya here would have no way of knowing if she had baby blues, since she's *always* depressed."

"Very funny," Tanya said.

"That sounds right," I said to Maxine. "Your hormones just need to balance out again, Crystal."

Crystal gave us both a look, then said, "This is way worse than that."

"How can anything be worse than that?" Tanya asked. "From what I hear, some women even feel suicidal after giving birth!"

"Oh, good one," Ships hissed. "You know just how to cheer a person up."

They began making faces at each other, so I flicked some ice water their way. "Could one of you please stay on task? We're here to help Crystal."

Tanya and Ships gave each other one last smirk, but quieted down.

Maxine shrugged and said, "A little rouge and some lipstick cures everything." Then she saw our disappointment in her offhand remark and said, "Or maybe not."

"It's like . . ." Crystal seemed almost afraid to tell us. "It's like . . . I don't want to be a mother anymore." She looked from face to face, seeing how that registered. "What's wrong with me?"

"Have you talked to Peter?" I asked.

Crystal nodded. "He doesn't know what to do, either. We're both sort of waiting for these feelings to pass, but . . . they just seem to be getting worse."

"Maybe it's like they say," Ships offered. "Once you have more kids than hands—it's a lot harder."

Crystal shook her head. "It isn't that. The boys are so sweet and helpful. Really, they are so loving toward her—"

"And you have relatives close by to help out," Maxine said.

"Oh, I do. And they're wonderful. One of my sisters is almost always willing to take the kids if I have to do something. Peter and I can still go out . . . it's not like I'm overburdened, honestly."

Our food arrived, and we all started eating, quietly thinking. *So what makes a bright, talented mother, with a great husband and three healthy children, feel unfulfilled?*

"Okay, let's go through the list," I said. "Remember at BYU? Whenever one of us felt bad, we'd take an inventory."

"I remember," Crystal said. "We'd always find something was missing that we should be doing. Let's see . . . personal prayer, scripture study, service, keep the commandments, temple attendance . . ." Crystal ticked each one off on a different finger. "Well, I'm not the greatest missionary . . ."

"Oh, please," Tanya said. "You are the perfect example. I'm surprised people aren't following you around begging to join whatever church you belong to."

Crystal laughed.

"Does Peter's calling take him away too much?" Maxine asked. Peter was a counselor in the bishopric.

"No, that's not it," Crystal said.

We didn't figure it out at that luncheon, but at least Crystal seemed to have a good time with us. That night, I asked Jonathan what he thought the problem could be.

"I think Crystal pushes herself too hard," Jonathan said. "She demands so much of herself, and she's expecting to bounce back too fast from this third pregnancy."

That sounded right to me, so I shared it at our next luncheon.

"That's true; you do demand a lot of yourself," Tanya agreed.

Crystal just shook her head. "It isn't that. Physically I feel fine. But mentally I'm just—" she searched for the word. "Lost."

Maxine squeezed her shoulders. "Oh, sweetie," she said.

"I've got it!" Ships shouted. "Not enough Italian food."

"You're a genius," I said. "To think there was such a simple solution, right under our noses."

Crystal's face suddenly changed, and she held up a hand. "Wait." We all watched her for a few seconds, as she thought. "That's it," she said triumphantly.

"What's it?" Maxine asked. "Somebody help the old lady get up to speed here."

"What Heather just said," Crystal said. "*Simple solution.*"

We all just stared, not a single clue among us.

"It made me flash back to chemistry class," Crystal said. "I've never gone back to school, and I never became a chemist."

We all began talking at once then, assuring her that her divine role as a mother was far more important. Chemistry would always be there later.

"No," Crystal said, shushing us. "I think I had forgotten who I was. I completely put that part of me aside."

"So you're quitting motherhood and becoming a scientist?" Tanya was still confused.

Crystal smiled her old smile again. "See? That's exactly what I thought—that I had to be all one or all the other, so I completely gave up chemistry. I thought that to be a good mother, I couldn't continue learning in my field."

"So what are you saying now?"

"I'm saying I can do both. It's brilliant. I don't have to pursue science full-time in a lab—I can just, you know, kick it around. Bring it back into my life again. I can read about it, I can teach it to my kids. It can be a visible part of me."

"That was always part of what made you Crystal," I said.

"It's what brought me joy," Crystal said. "And it still can." She was clicking along now. "Chemistry is all around us," she continued, now sounding like a tour guide in a museum. "And I'm going to enjoy it without feeling like I'm a bad mother."

"Of course you don't need to feel that," Maxine said. "It will make you an even better mother, because look how smart you can make your children."

"I could probably take one home study class a year and still get my degree. I don't know why I never thought of this before. I can't wait to tell Peter!"

I raised my water glass in a toast. "To Crystal," I shouted. "Come on, raise that H$_2$O."

## Mom's Chicken Soup

1 whole chicken
1 large onion, chopped
3/4 cup fresh parsley, chopped
3 ribs celery, including leaves, chopped
5 large carrots, sliced
1/2 cup cabbage, chopped
1/2 cup zucchini, chopped
1 cup wide noodles, cooked
1 teaspoon chicken bouillon
1 teaspoon salt
1/2 teaspoon pepper
1 bay leaf

Maxine's makeup might not cure anything, but this scrumptious soup can definitely make you feel better! It freezes well, too.

In large soup pot, boil chicken in 9 cups water, until tender and falling apart. Remove bones, skin, and gristle. Add remaining ingredients and simmer 1–3 hours. Remove bay leaf before serving.

Serves 10.

# Chapter 9

*Therefore shall a man leave his father and his mother, and shall cleave
unto his wife: and they shall be one flesh.*

Genesis 2:24

Every couple has to address the holiday issue sooner or later.
Which set of parents will they spend Christmas with, and which
one Thanksgiving, and then which one Easter? Otherwise well-
conceived holidays become dreaded powder kegs of family pres-
sures, hurt feelings, and burnt biscuits.

Jonathan and I decided to scrap the entire debate, and simply
invite everyone to our house for every holiday, every year.

"You're going to regret that," Tanya said, waving her fork at me
in between bites of salad.

"You'll be slaving away in the kitchen on every holiday," Ships
agreed.

"I know," I said. "But I can't have in-laws pouting and competing.
It's way less stressful to just have them over to our place. Besides, they
all live close by."

Maxine shrugged. "Well, don't say we didn't warn you. Sam
and I just went to Disneyland for everything."

Crystal laughed. "I think I like that idea. Then you can see
people at other times, when it's less pressure."

"Or not see them at all!" Maxine crowed. "Relatives can really
botch up a nice holiday."

"Oh, you said it," Crystal nodded. "Peter's mom is absolutely impossible. Honestly, you cannot win with that woman. Everything you do, she has a better way of doing it."

"Like the time she switched the socks on Christian? I'll never forget that," Ships said.

"What socks?" the rest of us asked.

"Oh. Get this," Crystal said. "I had just dressed Christian, and we're on the way to the zoo, right? So I buckle him in the back seat, and Andrew is in the front. Phyllis gets in back with Christian. And as we're driving there, I look in my rearview mirror, and Phyllis is taking off Christian's shoes. So I'm thinking, that's weird, I wonder why she's doing that, but I don't say anything, and then I see her *switching his socks.* Then she puts the shoes back on. And doesn't say a word about it."

"Just to have it her way," Ships added.

"It would kill her to let someone else be in charge," Crystal said. "She always has to have the last word."

"That is one uptight woman," Maxine said.

Our meals arrived and Crystal went on. "She stirs the food I'm cooking, she adjusts the oven temperature, she refolds my towels. I'm telling you, when I know a visit is coming up I almost break out in hives."

"Why don't you tell her to cut it out or you'll knock her block off?" Tanya asked. That is exactly how Tanya would probably handle it.

I laughed. "I can just see Crystal saying that to Peter's mom."

"I can only imagine the family rift that would cause," Crystal said.

"So let 'em rift," Tanya said. "You can't live like this, with that woman undermining everything you do. Next she'll be telling you how to raise your kids."

Crystal smiled weakly.

"Oh, she's already doing that?" Tanya asked. "Well, let her. Send 'em off to Grandma's and you go to Tahiti."

Crystal smiled and shook her head. "If only it were that easy. Hey, speaking of traveling, we haven't seen you at the last three luncheons."

Tanya smiled. "The Towers have been touring," she said in a thick British accent. "Places to go, people to see."

"Yeah, well, it stinks for the rest of us," Ships said. "Here I've been dying to go to Italy with Marco, and you beat me to it. And Heather, here, wants Jonathan to take her to Japan, but no, Tanya goes instead. What is it with you?"

Tanya lapped up the envy and smacked her lips. "Well, we have to keep reconciling, you know."

"That is unbelievable," Crystal said. "I think you keep your marriage on the rocks on purpose, just so you can make up after a fight and take a trip somewhere."

Tanya sighed and strummed her lacquered fingernails on the table. "Well, whatever works, girls."

We all groaned and booed, and Tanya held out her hands to silence us. "Hey. I'm the one with a bad marriage. You all got dream boys, so you can't begrudge me a little travel now and then."

"Something is wrong with the universe," I muttered, "when two people who don't even like each other end up spending all their time together in exotic locations."

"Well, it's not going to last forever," Tanya said. "Molly's two now, and I have to start hunting for a preschool."

"What's wrong with just taking her along on your trips?" I asked.

All of them stared at me. "Trips with your children are entirely different than trips you take alone," Ships said. "It is totally unromantic if the kids are hanging on you every minute."

"Absolutely," Tanya said. "Maybe that's why Preston and I can't enjoy our trips—because we're in parent mode instead of dating mode."

"Or," I said, rolling my eyes, "maybe you just don't like Preston."

Tanya smiled. "Yeah, that too."

I sighed. "So what preschools are you looking at?"

Tanya listed the ones Ships had used for her kids, and where Crystal was sending Andrew.

"But they're so fanatic about nutrition," Tanya said. "They won't even let you send a cookie in their lunch."

"Let alone a brownie, a bag of chips, and a candy bar," I teased.

Tanya grinned. "If that's what I happen to have on hand."

"How can you do that?" Crystal asked. "How can you let Molly eat just anything?"

Tanya gestured to Molly, asleep in her high chair, as if showing off a prized piece of art. "Ta da! Does this girl look deprived to you? She's off the chart! She's the healthiest kid in our whole group! While you guys are whirling your carrot juice, I'm opening a Twinkie and saying, 'Life is good, sugar pie, eat up.'"

We all shook our heads. "You're hopeless," Crystal laughed.

"Well, I don't remember anyone worrying this much about schools when I was your age," Maxine said. "There was one school in the neighborhood, and that's where they sent them. You girls have it much tougher now, with so many decisions to make."

"It's true," Ships said. "And there's so much pressure to get them reading early, playing soccer, taking karate—it's unbelievable."

We all nodded as Maxine said, "I think what kids need to do is watch the clouds go by now and then. Not that you don't teach them to work—that's important. But you need to let them be children, too. Not that I'm any expert." Maxine had finished her hamburger and was offering fries around the table now.

"But what about college entrance exams?" Crystal said.

We all scoffed and pelted her with "Give us a break," and "Worry about that later."

"No, seriously," Crystal said. And no one can be more serious than Crystal. "If they fall behind now, they'll stay behind. And the kids who have an edge will be the ones with the best SAT scores. They'll get all the scholarships."

"But if you pressure them too much they'll burn out," Ships said. "And they'll be miserable little robots, just trying to get scholarships."

Crystal's eyes narrowed. "Well, someone's going to get those scholarships. And I'll bet it won't be the kids who watched clouds all day!"

Now everyone was talking at once, until Maxine patted Crystal's arm and said, "Every one of you will know what's right for your own child. You're entitled to that inspiration. So, when Crystal prays about it, and Heather prays about it, and Tanya prays about it, and Ships prays about it—"

"We'll all get different answers," Crystal said. "You're right. And I'm sorry I said that about the clouds. I just feel this need to get my kids ready. It's so much more competitive than ever before . . ."

"Yes, it is," Maxine said. "All the more reason to listen to promptings from the Holy Ghost. These are big decisions."

We all thought about that. Finally Tanya broke the silence. "Well, I'm still giving Molly cookies."

"We knew you would," Ships said. "Glad to see you've made that decision prayerfully, too."

The waitress brought dessert menus, and Tanya snapped hers up. "How about dessert? Do I have to pray about what to have for dessert here?"

Maxine shook her head. "It will be interesting to see what happens twenty years from now. I hope I'll still be here to see it."

"Oh, of course you will be," we all assured her.

"You're younger than any of us in a lot of ways!" Crystal said.

Maxine threw her head back and laughed. "I'm so old, I remember when red, white, and blue was a novel color scheme."

We all laughed, then ordered a lemon tart with five forks.

"You have to be here," Tanya said to Maxine. "I'm counting on dumping Molly with you so I can travel some more."

"Then you have to watch my kids so I can join her," Crystal said.

"And mine," I added.

"And mine," Ships said. "See, this whole friendship thing is just a ruse to get you to watch our children for us."

Maxine laughed. "I'd be glad to," she said. And she actually meant it. "Send me a postcard from Singapore. I've always wanted to go there. I have no idea why."

"You'll make it," Ships said, looping her arm through Maxine's, and resting her head on her shoulder.

Sometimes Maxine joined one or the other of us for a family home evening, and always brought a homemade treat. She was delighted when our kids got old enough to try and teach the lessons, and applauded wildly when they finished. Of course, Gino and Francesca were already old enough to teach lessons, so Maxine went there most often.

* * *

"I signed up for my first correspondence class," Crystal announced at our next luncheon. "It might take me a few years, but I'm going to get that chemistry degree."

She was back to herself, glowing and confident. "You guys were right," she continued. "It feels so good just to know I'm taking some action."

"Hey." I nudged Ships. "We're a think tank now."

Ships rolled her eyes. "I'll have to tell Marco."

"And Peter is so relieved," Crystal said, buttering a pinch of bread. "He really had no idea how to help. And you know men— they want to solve the problem and rescue the maiden."

"Well, let's just be glad it wasn't something worse," Tanya said, "Like some chemical imbalance that makes those crazy mothers kill their kids or themselves."

We all just stared.

"I take back what I said about a think tank," I mumbled.

"Okay." Tanya acknowledged going over the top. "But seriously, there are aspects of parenting that make you nuts. Look at diapering, alone."

"Do you realize I have never changed a diaper?" Ships asked.

"Are you bragging or complaining?" Tanya asked.

Ships laughed. "I guess I am pretty lucky, huh? I came along just after all the yucky stuff was done."

"Oh, there's more yucky stuff in store, trust me," Tanya said. "Or am I the only one who still threw tantrums as a teenager?"

"Well, I'm not having teenagers," Ships said, taking a bite of her chicken Romana. "I'm locking them up when they turn thirteen, and not letting them out until they're twenty-one."

"This is cool for the rest of us, actually," I said. "You'll be the token pioneer woman, who forges ahead and goes through everything before the rest of us. So you can warn us of the pitfalls." Already Ships had helped Crystal through a high-chair purchase and preschool interviews.

"It's like when you're a little kid and you're exploring some creepy old abandoned house," Maxine said. "And you push your sister ahead of you, and say, 'You go first.'"

"Oh, great," Ships said. "I'm the guinea pig."

"Oh, I almost forgot," Crystal said, lifting a long, thin box up onto the table.

"You brought us roses?" Tanya said. "Ooh-la-la."

"Nope," Crystal smiled. "Something better."

We had all finished eating, so we pushed our plates aside to make room for the box. Crystal stood with her hand on the lid to set the scene for her surprise. "Now, I know some of us feel we're through having babies . . ."

"Well, she's got me pegged," Maxine said.

"Will you just open the box already?" Ships asked.

"Just a minute, here. This is important." Crystal cleared her throat. "But in case any other babies are born within our little group, we all want to be prepared."

She lifted the lid, and there in the box were five glittering wands, wrapped with ribbons and feathers, and topped with twinkly stars. "These are our official wands!"

We all clapped and cheered, grabbing the wands and bopping each other on the heads with them.

"I give you the gift of today's check," Tanya said, as she waved her wand over Ships.

"And you get a sense of humor," Ships said.

"Won't these be adorable next time one of us has a baby?"

"What about the children who didn't get gifts yet? We need to do them retroactively," Maxine said. "Let's see, I give Gino . . . what can you give that kid? He's got everything! Those huge brown eyes, that big smile . . ."

JONI HILTON

"He's gonna need a distraction from the ladies who'll be throwing themselves at him," Tanya said. "Give him athletic ability."

Ships laughed, pleased with Gino's admiration club.

"Perfect," Maxine said, waving her wand. "And Francesca will get . . ."

"Let her have an insatiable urge to clean the house," Ships suggested.

"Yeah, give that to all our kids," I agreed.

"I decree that she'll become a mother herself one day, and give you lots of grandchildren," Maxine smiled.

Ships laughed. "I'll get them one way or another, huh?"

"Well, you guys will have to be the Labor Ladies from now on. I feel very much done, thank you very much," Tanya said.

"Oh, you can't quit after Molly," Maxine said. "She's so adorable; don't you want another one so cute?"

Tanya smiled and thanked her for the compliment, but then said, "No."

A woman across the aisle kept glancing over at our noisy group, and finally Crystal said to her, "What must people think of us when we come to a restaurant? 'Are they crazy? They have all these babies and they're waving all these wands . . .'"

The woman and her companion smiled, and she said, "That's not what prevents pregnancy, you know."

We all laughed at that, waved our wands again just for fun, and then mercifully left the other diners alone.

* * *

"You need a group like this," I told Jonathan that night.

"What, you want me to befriend a bunch of crazy guys who can't figure out the check, and who smack each other with sticks?"

I put my hands on my hips. "That is not what we do," I said. "These wands are the cutest things ever. I think Crystal made them herself."

"Someone needs to get a life . . ."

"No, she does not. She has a life. She has three kids now, plus chemistry."

Jonathan looked at me sideways. "Chemistry? With Peter?"

I couldn't help laughing, falling backward on the bed. "No, not with Peter!" I went into another fit of laughter, as Jonathan stood staring at me.

"I'm waiting to hear who she's having chemistry with."

"Nobody! You nut—she was a chemistry major! So she has that—her interest in chemistry, plus being a mother. No wonder you men don't have luncheon groups—I can just imagine the miscommunications. That's because men are always thinking of one thing."

Jonathan smiled, and nodded. "Ah. So that's what you think."

"Well, it's true," I smiled, slithering off the bed.

"And it's the furthest thing from *your* mind, right?"

I giggled and ran into the kitchen, and Jonathan came after me. I laughed, falling into his arms. "Okay, I'll admit it. But my visiting teachers are coming over in five minutes."

"Visiting teachers? Have they ever come over at a convenient time?" Jonathan asked. "Ever once?"

I sighed. "No. But we can't let them know that. They're just trying to do their job. They don't know they're coming at odd times. I mean, they do set up appointments . . ."

"Just as I get home from work?"

Just then the doorbell rang. I swung it wide open and greeted them with a big smile. "Welcome! We were just talking about you," I said, ushering them inside and winking at Jonathan behind their backs.

"Oh, there's Hayley," Sister Timmons said, noticing Hayley sitting on a blanket, playing with her plush rabbit. "She is so cute."

"*Muy bonita.* She's much prettier than the other babies her age," Sister Sanchez added.

"I like these women," Jonathan said. "They have excellent judgment."

They laughed, and settled down on the sofa. Jonathan went down the hall to his office.

"Today we want to tell you about the importance of friendships," Sister Timmons said. They went on to describe how vital it is for women to reach out to those around them, and form bonds.

Jonathan popped up into a window behind them, and wiggled his eyebrows.

"We can gain so much from our female associations," Sister Sanchez said with her faint Spanish accent. "We get busy with our husbands and children, but we must also remember to serve those around us . . ."

Again Jonathan popped up with the eyebrows.

I started giggling. "I'm sorry," I said. "I guess I'm just laughing because I went out to lunch today with some girlfriends—the very thing you're talking about."

"Good for you," Sister Timmons said. "Women can be a great source of knowledge and support, especially in the child-rearing years."

It had become almost impossible to ignore Jonathan, who was now making faces, and hitting himself on the head with the wand I brought home from lunch, then making googly eyes. Sister Sanchez and Sister Timmons took turns reading from the *Ensign* about the value of women supporting each other.

"Sometimes we just get together and laugh," I said, still trying to control my own laughter.

Now Jonathan was behind the window waving a purse, and letting his wrist go limp, pretending to be chatting away with an invisible friend.

"That's good, too," Sister Sanchez said. "And even now you are laughing."

"Yes, well," I said, struggling to stop, "it just kind of . . . lasts . . ."

"Well, you are a very happy lady," Sister Sanchez said. "And that is good."

They stood to leave.

"Oh, yes," I said. "Very good." I saw them to the door, biting my cheeks to keep from busting up laughing again. "Thank you for coming by." My voice was a squeak now.

"Are you sure you're all right?" Sister Timmons asked.

"Oh, fine. Really. Just fine." I was nodding like a parade horse now, emphasizing my answer, and finally closed the door.

I whirled around to the window, but Jonathan was gone. I went to his office, where he had run back inside and was pretending to be busy with paperwork.

He was laughing so hard he was wheezing now, and my scolding only made it funnier to him.

"You ruined their visit," I snapped.

"I was just enacting what they were saying," he said. "How you ladies are when you get together."

"That was not funny," I said, trying desperately not to laugh, myself. "I wish they had seen you. That would have served you right."

Now Jonathan was wiping tears from his eyes, winding down from his hysterics. "Oh, that was a priceless moment."

Then he pulled me close and kissed me. "I knew you were good for laughs, but I didn't realize you had helpers . . ."

Hayley was gurgling now, so I smacked Jonathan and went back into the living room. "Let's make dinner," I said to her, swinging her up into my arms and heading into the kitchen. "What would Mama's girl like to eat tonight? Would you like oven-baked ribs?"

I strapped her into her high chair, then started pulling things out of the pantry and stacking them on the counter. "How about spaghetti? Or corn—would you like corn with a little piece of ham? We have ham . . . how about tuna? With some pickle relish? Yum, yum, Hayley. How about—"

Suddenly Jonathan was behind me and pulled me around into a huge hug.

"I love you so much," he whispered into my hair. "Just look at what a cute mom you are. She is so lucky . . ."

I pulled back a few inches. "But . . . it's just . . . food."

"It's the way you do it," Jonathan said. "It makes me fall in love with you all over again."

I smiled and we kissed. "Do you love me enough to make dinner?"

Jonathan smiled back. "Nope."

I laughed. "Just as I thought." I went back to the pantry. "Or there's some soup, Hayley . . ."

"Let's go out to dinner instead," Jonathan said, twirling me by my hand.

"Oh, now you a-speakin' my lingo," I said. Then I turned to Hayley, "We like that idea, don't we, honey?"

I started down the hall with her. "I'll throw on a diaper and some lipstick and we're good to go."

"Gee, the image that creates . . ." Jonathan said.

"Just think," I shouted from the bedroom, "that's probably what old people actually say."

Jonathan was rolling his eyes as I came back out. "I can hardly wait."

# Baked Barbecued Ribs

3 pounds country-style pork ribs
3/4 cup ketchup
1/3 cup maple syrup
2 Tablespoons cider vinegar
1 Tablespoon bottled steak sauce
1 Tablespoon Dijon mustard
1 teaspoon cinnamon
1/2 teaspoon allspice
1/4 teaspoon black pepper
1/8 teaspoon cloves
Dashes of Tabasco sauce, to taste

All our husbands like this recipe. Jonathan likes the ribs served with a side of Funeral Potatoes (which I'm sure you already know how to make), and a crisp green salad. Here's how to make them:

Line a shallow roasting pan with foil. Place ribs in pan, bone-side up. Bake at 350 degrees for 1 hour.

While ribs bake, heat all remaining ingredients to boiling in small saucepan. Reduce heat and simmer uncovered for 15 minutes.

Take ribs out of oven. Drain off fat and turn them meaty side up.

Spoon half the sauce over ribs. Bake 45–60 minutes more, until ribs are tender. Add the remaining sauce during last 15 minutes of cooking.

Serves 4.

# Chapter 10

*Trust in the Lord with all thine heart; and lean not
unto thine own understanding.*
Proverbs 3:5

Young teenage girls have no idea how valuable they are. Beyond their eternal value as defined in the Young Women's program, they are right-this-minute valuable to countless couples who need babysitters. If these girls were traded on the stock market, the ones in my neighborhood alone could triple the trading day.

"You're like gold!" I beamed at Jessica when she came over the first time. We had usually asked one of the sets of grandparents to watch Hayley when we went to the temple or had a special date, but this time they weren't available, so we dove into the pool of frantic parents making phone calls.

"I can't believe I got you," I said. "I hear you're almost always booked on a Friday night."

Jessica chuckled. "The Barstows had to cancel their plans, and you called just after that."

*Before word got out! Yes! Perfect timing.* The minute a block of time became available, swarms of vulture parents would descend to fight over it. It was worse than trying to get into EFY.

But this time Jonathan and I had beat out the competition, and Jessica was ours until 11:00. We were thrilled, and soon found ourselves in the temple parking lot, just in time for the 8:00 session.

For two glorious hours, we left the concerns of the world behind us, and stepped into the peace and serenity of the temple. Sweet little white-haired temple workers with crinkly eyes smiled at me as if I were the first person they'd seen that day. The feeling there was such a contrast to the outside world; I wanted to stay forever.

When our session was almost finished, a new group of veil workers was escorted in to help with our large group. And there was Maxine! I so hoped I would get her, and my heart soared when I did.

I squeezed her hand and thought, *This is how it will be. We'll always have each other.* We both started crying, but we got through the ceremony, and met again in the celestial room.

Jonathan was glad to see her, too. Suddenly, I had such a clear impression I gasped.

"I knew it!" Maxine whispered. "I felt something when I was helping you at the veil. You're going to have a baby, aren't you?"

I looked at Jonathan, who registered absolute shock.

Then I turned back to Maxine and nodded. "I think so. I think the Spirit just told me."

"Do you mean it?" Jonathan asked, turning to embrace me.

I could only nod, as tears slid down my cheeks.

Maxine was crying, too, and soon Jonathan was as well. I knew this was going to be an exceptional child.

"I feel so blessed," Maxine said. "The Lord didn't give me any babies, but every once in awhile, he lets me be the first to know about someone else's."

I hugged her and kissed her cheek. I loved her so much at that instant, I wanted to name my baby after her.

"Looks like you girls will need another luncheon," Jonathan said.

He was right. I waited a couple of weeks until the doctor could confirm it, but then I called the gang and asked them to meet at Friday's.

"It's definite," I said, waving my pregnancy results around the table. They all cheered. Even people at other tables were cheering for us.

"We have baby cakes," the waiter said in a thick accent.

"Oh, baby cakes!" we all squealed, like we never get out.

"Yes, bring each of us one," Ships said.

"This is too fun," Tanya said. "And I have some great news, too. You're never going to believe this, but I landed a film!"

"A film? You're going to be in a movie?" Crystal asked.

"Yup. It's a small, independent film, but a great script," Tanya said. "I play a female cop and I get to arrest the star of the movie. Who is Mr. Hunk himself, Zachary Hannigan."

"No way!" we all shouted, then cheered again.

"Zachary Hannigan, who's he?" Maxine asked. We all filled her in on the dishy roles he'd played on soap operas and TV movies, always the suave charmer.

"Do you get to kiss him?" Ships asked.

"Of course not," Tanya said. "I'm arresting him. Hello?"

Ships shrugged. "So what? Anything can happen in the movies."

"Well, that's a bit of a stretch," Tanya laughed. "But I'll be on the set with him, and that's cool enough for me!"

"You'll finally be a movie star," I said, high-fiving her.

"Well, not exactly a star," Tanya said. "It's a pretty small part."

"But you're there, you're in it," I argued. "That makes you a star."

They all agreed, and we cheered for Tanya again.

"When does it shoot?" Ships asked.

"In six months, down in L.A. So I won't even have to travel far."

"Sounds perfect," Crystal said. "We'll all come to the premiere."

"You got it," Tanya said. "Plus, Molly will be in preschool then, and Preston can pick her up."

"Yay, Preston!" Crystal shouted, then noticed no one else was cheering for him, and put her water glass down. "Well, it is good that he can do that," she said.

"He's a peach," Tanya yawned.

"Well, he does teach a lovely Family Home Evening lesson," Maxine said, on Preston's behalf.

Tanya laughed. "Yes he does, doesn't he? I'll tell you what, though. It is totally impossible to be an active member of this

Church and lose weight. And I'll tell you why. Family home evening. Every single week you have treats and desserts thrust in front of you, and how are you supposed to diet?"

We were all laughing, and Tanya went on. "They make it impossible. And then people wonder why there are so many fat Mormon women. I'm telling you, it's because of family home evening."

"It's all a diabolical plot to keep us fat," I said.

"Well it *could* be," Tanya said, getting wound up. "I mean, why does there have to be sugar in everything? Refreshments after every meeting? Goodies in every class? What is it—some kind of pay-off to C&H Sugar?"

"Let's see, weren't you the woman who was arguing about your right to send sugary snacks to preschool with Molly?"

"That's different. That's because she likes them."

"Well," Crystal said, "we like refreshments."

"You know," Maxine said, "It's kind of like the Garden of Eden, when God gave Adam and Eve two conflicting commandments. And now he's telling us to obey the Word of Wisdom, yet have family home evening." She looked at us as if she had just unveiled another Dead Sea Scroll.

"So we're in the Garden of Eatin'," I said. They all groaned.

Tanya shook her head. "I give up. There is no diet that can get you around family home evening."

"Have carob," I suggested. For that I was pummeled with menus.

"Carob tastes terrible! We might as well have soy bars."

"Okay, okay, I was just trying to help."

We finally concluded that Tanya should have moderation in all things, including her family home evening snack. Thus, when the treat was Rice Crispy Bars, she was to have one Rice Crispy.

Tanya sighed. "I don't know why I'm so worked up about it. I eat sweet rolls for breakfast half the time."

"What?"

"You made us go through that whole discussion for nothing?"

"You're not even dieting?"

"No dessert for you," Ships said, taking away Tanya's menu.

"None for me, either," I said. "Morning sickness."

We spent the next fifteen minutes repeating our morning sickness stories: how the only thing Crystal could stand was olives, how Tanya always craved watermelon, and how the only thing I could keep down was Pop Tarts. And a yummy seafood casserole I learned to make from Jonathan's mother.

"See?" I nudged Ships. "Another unpleasantry you got to miss."

Ships smiled. "You have a point."

* * *

That Sunday I noticed Tanya wasn't at church. She and Preston had moved into our ward three months before, and I had always looked forward to seeing her across the chapel. So I called that afternoon.

"Mmyeah." The voice was Tanya's, but the flat, slurry greeting was weird.

"Is this Tanya?" I asked.

"It's me," she said. "I really don't want to talk."

"What?" I said. "I'll come right over."

Jonathan watched as I threw a jacket on. "How is it that if someone doesn't want to talk, women assume they want company? Isn't that talking plus seeing someone?"

"Trust me," I said, kissing Jonathan, and then the top of Hayley's head as I dashed out the door. "Something serious is going on."

Tanya answered in a bathrobe, bleary-eyed from crying, with a box of Kleenex under one arm. Preston was in the kitchen feeding Molly, and waved as he saw me walk by.

"What's happened?" I asked. Tanya and I sat down in the den, and Tanya closed the door.

"I can't do the movie," she said.

"What? Why not? Did it have an inappropriate scene or someth—"

"Nope," Tanya said, leaning back limply in her chair.

"What, then? Does Preston not want you to—"

"Nope." Tanya sighed.

"Well, then, tell me."

She sat up, burst into a new round of tears, and said, "I'm pregnant!"

I wanted to throw my arms around her. "That's wonderful, honey! Why are you crying?"

"Because filming starts in six months!" she wailed. "I'll be eight months pregnant! Do you think they're going to have a big, pregnant cop arresting the star of the movie?"

"Oh my gosh," I whispered. "When did you find out?"

"Yesterday," she said. "At lunch you guys were talking about watermelon, and I realized I hadn't had my period in a few weeks, so I went to the doctor, and whammo! End of film career."

"Oh, Tanya." I went over to her and held her for a few minutes. Here was an exciting event, the birth of a child, and here was its mother, furious. There would be no convincing Tanya to see this as anything but a disaster.

"Why me? Why me?" Tanya was hitting the cushion now, as devastated as Ships had been when she'd found out she *couldn't* have children. I thought of pointing that out. I thought of reminding Tanya of the reason why we're here in this life. I thought about telling her she'd feel totally different once she looked into the eyes of that new little soul . . . but I could tell Tanya was not open to anything right now but rage.

"There will be other movies," I said at last.

"I'm getting older all the time," Tanya said through a soggy tissue. "Chances like this are—"

"Have you prayed about it? Maybe this is God's will that a special little perso—"

Tanya laughed bitterly and started pacing. "You think God wanted this? God wants me to be a complete failure as an actress? I get one chance—one chance, Heather! And look what He does to me."

"You're not even thirty," I said. "This is the best time for you to be having children—"

"With him?" Tanya hissed, pointing toward the closed doors. "Like I want another baby with *Preston?*" She fairly spat his name out.

"Sit down," I said. "You need to see the whole picture."

"The whole picture is that I had my chance, Heather, and now it's gone. I have a lousy marriage, a lousy life. And it's about to get worse."

This time I didn't say anything. I wanted to go into the kitchen, grab Molly, and take her to a timeless fairyland, where everything was pink and white, everyone adored her, and she would never have to hear one shrill voice. I wanted to pull Tanya's baby from her stomach, hand it back to Heavenly Father, and see that it got placed with a loving mother. I wanted to slap Tanya and shout, "Places, everybody! Take One!"

Quietly, but resolutely, I stood up and said, "I think I'm too angry to stay here any longer," and headed for the front door.

"Wait!" Tanya grabbed my sleeve and turned me around. "Don't go. Please. You're the only one who will listen to me."

"No," I said. "I'm one of the ones who won't, Tanya. I can't listen to you throwing dirt on what I believe. I can't do it." I turned again.

"Who will I talk to?" Tanya screamed as I headed out.

"Talk to God," I said, then slammed the door and muttered to myself, "for once."

* * *

When I stomped through the door Jonathan had Hayley on his lap, and looked up from their storybook. He could tell from my face that things were not good, but he could also tell that I needed some time alone, so he finished the book, then put Hayley on a blanket with some toys to keep her busy.

"What happened?"

I was splashing water on my face and patting it with a towel in the bathroom. "I swear she's gonna burn in hell one day," I said.

Jonathan leaned against the counter. "Oh, so you had a nice visit."

I sighed, socked him gently for his joke, then leaned against his chest. "She's pregnant," I said.

"You're kidding! Well, great!"

"No. She's mad about it because now she can't be in that movie."

Jonathan rested his chin on my head, thinking, then pulled away. "I hope you talked some sense into her."

"Nope. I just got fed up with it and left. I couldn't take it anymore. She is so self-centered, Jonathan. I can't believe God even sent that perfect little Molly to her."

"He does work in mysterious ways." Jonathan smiled. "Hey, she just got the news, her hormones are going crazy, she's an actress—" He shrugged. "She'll calm down. Next time you see her she'll be glowing and picking out baby names."

I sighed and leaned back against the mirror. "Yeah, well, I'm busy that day."

"What—you're throwing in the towel? You guys have been friends for almost twenty years! You can't just give up on her."

"I can if she turns into a jerk."

Jonathan crossed his arms, still smiling. "Don't you guys have some kind of lifelong promise?"

"Oh, that was just stupid. It was in the fifth grade, for heaven's sake."

"Ah, ah, ah," Jonathan said, as if checking the Promise Rules. "You would be friends 'forever,' I believe?"

I shook my head. "Wanting a movie part over a baby, Jonathan? Is that not sick? Talk about leaning unto your own understanding instead of God's. She's leaning so far she's stumbled over it and landed flat on her face."

Jonathan took my hands. "So, when does someone most need a friend? When everything's going well? When they're thinking straight? When life is easy?"

I sighed.

"She needs you now more than ever, Heather."

I knew he was right, and twisted out of his arms. "Oh, fine!" I growled. I grabbed my car keys and headed out again.

Tanya answered the door again, and I pushed my way in. "Okay, you stupid jerk," I said. "I'll listen. But only because I promised in the fifth grade that—" and then I couldn't say another word. I simply threw my arms around Tanya and cried. She cried, too, and as Preston carried little Molly up to bed, we stood there in the entryway, sobbing on one another's shoulders.

"You're being so selfish," I cried. "I'm so mad at you!"

"I don't know how else to be," Tanya yelled back through her tears.

"Well maybe that's why God keeps sending you babies, you big idiot," I snarled, "so you'll finally learn."

Tanya started laughing. Both of us collapsed on the sofa, laughing and crying.

"I hate you," I said.

"No, you love me," Tanya said. "That's why you came back over. Look, I know I'm wrong. I know I should be thrilled about the new baby. It's just that—"

"Just that what?"

Now Tanya reached into her heart, took out the paltry contents, and laid them on the table. In the smallest voice I've ever heard, Tanya said, "I guess I just wanted to be famous."

I took her in my arms and stroked her hair. "Oh, Tanya. If you only knew how famous you are to your children. And their children. And to God. If it's approval you want . . . you're looking in all the wrong places."

Tanya pulled back, almost timidly. "I've never told anyone that," she said. "Please don't tell anybody. It's sounds so shallow now that I've actually said it."

I held her to me. "Never be ashamed of honesty," I whispered. I looked into her eyes and brushed a tear away with my thumb. "Remember when Satan came to tempt Christ? One of the things he tempted him with was fame."

"It was?" Tanya sighed. "I wasn't the best seminary student."

"Most people want some kind of fame," I said. "That can be popularity, prestige, some kind of public recognition . . ."

"So it's natural," Tanya said.

"It's the natural man we have to overcome," I said. "We have to seek God's approval instead of man's. That's what Jesus was trying to teach us. And I'm not saying it's wrong to be famous, Tanya. What matters is if your heart is in the right place. You have to make God's priorities your priorities."

Tanya nodded. "And He's giving me another chance."

I smiled. "Will you pray about this baby? Please?"

"I will," she said, and clasped my hands in hers. "Thank you, Heather. It's so hard, though."

"I know." Then I tipped her chin up. "Life's hard for everybody, Tanya. That's by design. And that's why we need each other."

She walked me to the door with her arm slung around my shoulders. "Maybe I'll name this baby after you," she said.

I smiled. "And if it's a boy?"

"Hmm. What would be the masculine form of Heather? I know—Heathen."

"Ah. I can hardly wait," I said, shaking my head and stepping down her stairs. "Read your scriptures," I shouted as I got into the car.

"I will!" She waved from the porch.

# Seafood Casserole

Wonderful served over rice. Great for company, too.

1 rib celery, chopped
1 cup onion, finely chopped
1/2 cup butter (1 stick)
1/2 cup flour
1 (13-ounce) can evaporated milk (not condensed)
2 egg yolks, beaten
1 teaspoon salt
1/2 teaspoon red pepper
1 pound raw crab meat, shrimp, or other seafood
1/2 pound cheddar cheese, grated

Jonathan's mom taught me how to make this dish, which was lucky, or I might have starved during my first pregnancy.

Sauté celery and onion in butter until wilted. Blend in flour and milk gradually. Whisk in eggs; stir continually. Add seafood; cook for 5 minutes. Pour into casserole dish, top with cheddar cheese, and bake at 375 degrees for 10–15 minutes.

Serves 6.

# Chapter 11

*He maketh the barren woman to keep house, and to be
a joyful mother of children . . .*
Psalms 113:9

"And you think she isn't spoiled," Jonathan said when he came home one night and found Hayley wearing a crown, waving a wand, and sitting in her bouncy chair under a cardboard castle doorway.

I looked at the scene and laughed. "Well, she is a little princess," I said, grabbing the camera. "After all, she looks just like the king."

Jonathan rolled his eyes. "Your mom was here today, I take it."

My parents had grandkids from my two brothers, but they both lived farther away, so Hayley got the lion's share of their attention, and Mom couldn't resist bringing her lavish gifts on occasion—in this case, a giant play castle.

"She can't even walk yet," Jonathan said, pretending to be put out, but smiling at the playhouse.

"She doesn't need to walk," I said. "She just needs to sit on her throne and be pampered. Don't you, Hayley? 'Yes, I do,'" I cooed.

"She has the entire family wrapped around her little finger," Jonathan said, lifting her out of her chair.

"Especially her daddy," I agreed.

Hayley smiled, and a droplet of drool fell down onto Jonathan's shirt.

"Tanya and I both had our eight-month check-ups today," I said. "It's so funny, being pregnant along with her, and comparing notes. Hers are always more dramatic, of course."

"Of course." Jonathan rubbed my stomach. "But the doctor said everything's okay?"

"Yep. They're running blood tests, but the baby seems to be growing fine."

Tanya had come home with reports of the nurses chiding her about not shaving her legs, and the doctor chiding her about gaining so much weight.

"So stop eating and shave," I teased.

"Plus they keep saying maybe it will be twins," Tanya said.

"That's just to see you flip out—you give them a good show," I said. "I'll bet the nurses beg to work on the days when Tanya Towers has her appointments."

"I'll bet not," Tanya said. "I'll bet they call me Sasquatch behind my back."

"Why don't you shave, for heaven's sake?"

"It's too hard when you're this big around," Tanya said. "It's like I have a beach ball in the way."

It was good to hear Tanya chatting along about it without bursting into tears. She was even planning an outer space nursery theme.

"But won't that mean all the walls are black?" Crystal asked at our next luncheon.

"Not black, just kind of a dark blue," Tanya said.

Ships frowned. "You can't paint a baby's room like that. It'll look depressing."

"But it's a boy," Tanya said. "It will look masculine."

"Why not just buy him a fake mustache?" Ships said. "Babies don't need to be masculine that early. I say dark blue is a bad choice."

"And I say we ask the artist," Tanya snapped, then turned to me, smiling with confidence that I would back her up. "Won't it look striking and dramatic? And be educational?"

I looked back and forth from Ships to Tanya. "Well . . ."

"Oh, she's waffling," Tanya said. "We can't listen to her."

"Why not make it outer space in the daytime?" Maxine suggested. "Then it can be bright and sunny, with clouds and such."

We all looked at Maxine.

"Outer space in the *daytime?*" Crystal said. "Oh, geez."

"Maybe if you paint enough planets and rocket ships on the wall, you'll have mostly bright colors and just a little of the blue in the background," I said.

Tanya scowled.

"Why are you so dead-set on this outer space theme in the first place?" Ships asked.

"Because I found this really cute wastebasket shaped like a rocket," she mumbled.

"Oh, well, then! You absolutely must go with a space theme," I laughed.

"Just do a sports theme," Crystal said. "That's what it will end up as, anyway." Her boys were sharing a room filled with sports equipment, balls, and team flags.

Tanya took a bite of her crab-and-avocado sandwich, then said, "I'll see what Preston thinks."

We were all dumbfounded. This was the first time Tanya had ever expressed an interest in Preston's opinion. We usually envisioned her gritting her teeth through every day, trying to avoid him as much as possible. But here was some evidence that they were actually functioning as a team. I looked around the table, and everyone was smiling.

"Well, I'm getting pretty sick of the Italian theme, myself," Ships said.

At that, we all stared. "How can you get sick of Italian, when you married an Italian?" Crystal asked.

Ships sighed. "It's just so . . . I don't know."

"Hey," Tanya said, pointing to Ships's plate. "Ships ordered Asian salad." Tanya made emergency siren sounds.

"What's the matter?" Maxine asked.

Ships frowned. "Oh, it's just that . . . it's like when you travel and you finally get sick of someplace and you want to go home."

"Except that you are home," I said, softly, trying to break the news gently.

"I know," she said. "And when Marco and I got married, I was so happy about the whole Italian thing—you know, the passion, the romance, the food—"

"So what's not to like?"

"I'm just not sure I fit in. I mean, I'm English and Irish."

I chuckled. "Who really cares what nationality your ancestors were?" I asked. "I mean, I'm mostly Danish, but it's not like it forms a cultural clash with Jonathan's English background. It's not like I identify with some kind of Danish mind-set."

"I'm Polish," Maxine said. "Polish and Hungarian, I think. Or maybe it's Scottish, because I'm so thrifty."

"See?" I said. "It doesn't really matter."

"But it does in the Bonetti household," Ships said. "Being Italian is a big part of his identity. And the kids. It's like I can never top his first wife, because she'll always be a native Italian, and I'm, like, this grafted-on outsider."

"Ah," Maxine said. "You're worried about the first wife."

Ships nodded. "It's true. She's always there, you know? She's in the kids, she's in the cooking. It's like I'm just filling in."

"So bring in the Irish side," Tanya said. "Do some Irish cooking, and play up the other part of your family. Get Heather's recipe for scones."

"But I'm the only one," Ships said. "It feels stupid. Like I'm forcing some foreign culture onto them. And, really, I don't even identify with the Irish that much. I just want to be . . . nothing. You know, not have a culture per se."

"I still think you're worried about Isabella," Maxine said. "You feel like a replacement."

"I really do," Ships said. "Like I'm babysitting."

"Okay," Tanya said, smoothing out the table as if heading up a board meeting. "Let's look at the wife issue. Does Marco compare the two of you?"

"No. I mean, he probably goes out of his way not to bring her up, or to reminisce, even though I'm sure he has fond memories he'd like to share . . ."

"Do the kids make you feel second best?" Crystal asked.

"Hmm. Not really. They're honestly great kids."

"Then it's you," I said. "You're doing this yourself, just from your own insecurities."

Ships listened, then nodded. "Yeah, maybe so. It's like I'm so sure she was better than me."

Now we all groaned and began talking at once, telling Ships to believe in herself, that she's a wonderful woman, that Isabella was probably up in heaven jumping for joy when Marco picked such a great mother for their kids.

"You must believe in yourself," Maxine said. "You have every ability you need. Heavenly Father has given all of us the talents we need for the challenges we have in life. Didn't you know that?"

I glanced at Tanya, who seemed more surprised by this than Ships did.

"I guess that's true," Ships said, "But I keep thinking she was just more . . . Italian."

"Hey. If being Italian was essential, he wouldn't have married you in the first place," I said. "Obviously it's not as important to him as you think."

"That's right," Crystal said. "I'll bet if you just talk to him about it, he'll assure you that you're worried for nothing."

Ships sipped her cranberry juice. "Yeah, probably. Maybe I just need more assurance. But that sounds so . . . weak."

"So what?" Tanya said. "Never be ashamed of honesty." She glanced at me and smiled. "Just tell him you need more compliments. More validation."

"Yeah. Maybe he just doesn't realize how uneasy I feel. I mean, he and the kids speak Italian and mine's pretty rough."

"But you're cute rough," I said. "You're the adorable one who's trying to embrace their culture, but you still have your great American style."

"That's right!" Maxine said. "Look at all you bring to this family that his first wife couldn't have!"

"Yeah," Crystal agreed. "I'll bet she never made corn dogs. Or hamburgers. And look at you—you even make Italian breadsticks."

Ships laughed. "You guys have a good point. Maybe I've been trying to lose myself in this whole new identity. Maybe my own was okay before."

"Of course it was," Maxine said. "You're an American!" Maxine is possibly the most patriotic woman in America, and wears a flag pin on her lapel with pride. "Don't ever try to be anything else. Thank heavens we had lunch today—you could have been disinfected."

We all laughed at that, and Maxine shrugged. "Oh, you know what I mean."

Dessert arrived, and Crystal said, "You know, we actually have a culture all our own, being LDS."

"That's true," I agreed. "If you're old enough, you can remember resin grapes."

"Oh my gosh," Tanya said, almost choking on her ice water, "there are so many things that are just LDS. Stake houses, nineteen-year-old 'elders,' road shows, fast meetings that go so slow—who else would understand all that?"

"I still have my green Primary band-lo," I said. "I remember being a Firelight."

"Me too!" Ships shouted. "And remember two-and-a-half-minute talks?"

"You girls have nothing on me," Maxine said. "I went to Gold and Green Balls."

"Did you have green Jello?" Ships said.

"Of course." Maxine held her arms out. "I'm Jello-basted," she said.

That launched a whole new discussion about good things to baste chicken in, then good things to soak with in the bathtub, then good ingredients for a facial mask, then how scary we all look in facial masks, then Halloween masks, and finally, what our little babies were going to be that Halloween.

"Christian and Andrew are going as Tweedledee and Tweedledum, and Ashley's going to be Alice in Wonderland," Crystal said.

"Let me guess," Tanya sneered. "You've already sewn the costumes."

"Of course," Crystal grinned.

Tanya turned to me, "And I don't suppose our dress designer here bought a costume off the rack, either."

"Nope," I said. "Hayley is going to be a fairy princess, wearing a Heather Bench original."

"You people are disgusting," Tanya said, twirling her straw. "I have no talents whatsoever—"

"Oh, yeah," Ships said, as all of us chimed in to remind her of the many plays she had starred in. "Why don't you just use rayon for all your play costumes? Then when you wash them, they'll shrink so you can use them for Halloween costumes for Molly."

"Brilliant," Tanya replied. "Because you never want to wash stage costumes, otherwise."

Ships shrugged. "How do I know?"

"So let's see," Tanya said. "Molly could be a killer peasant. I don't think that would damage a kid's psyche too much."

"What did you go as, when you were little?" Maxine asked.

We all shared our stories of tripping over sheets and burlap bags in our homemade costumes of the sixties. Ships said she had usually frozen, wearing her marching parade outfits, and Crystal had always worn whatever cowgirl costume her big sister had worn the year before. I remembered being a clown with so much grease makeup on that by the time I got home, I looked like a Modigliani painting.

"I wore a long red wig and frosted pink lipstick, and went as Ann-Margret one year," Tanya said. "And not one person guessed right, who I was."

We all laughed.

"Those were the days," Maxine recalled, "before everyone started dressing so scary. I just hate the gruesome costumes. I don't give any candy unless the trick-or-treater is cute. And if they're very, very cute, I give them double."

That was so Maxine, we all had to laugh.

The check came, and we divvied it up. Just before we rose to leave, Tanya suddenly grabbed Crystal's arm in a death clutch.

"You guys!" she hissed. "My water just broke."

"Oh, saints in heaven," Maxine said. "We're gonna have another one."

"Hey, good timing," I teased her. "You waited until after dessert."

Ships and Crystal grabbed napkins from the next table, and we hurried Tanya to her car. "You sure you can make it home?" Maxine asked. "Let me drive you."

"No, no—I only live half a mile away," Tanya said. "I'll call you from the hospital."

We all followed her home in a caravan of four grinning women behind one grimacing one, and made sure Preston was on his way before we left. I scooped up Molly and took her home with me. Then I sat with my belly on my legs and thought, "Well, when will it be my turn?"

# Garlic Cheese "Italian" Breadsticks

1 package yeast
1/3 cup warm water
1 cup flour
1 Tablespoon oregano
1 Tablespoon shortening
1 teaspoon sugar
3/4 teaspoon salt
1/8 teaspoon garlic powder
1 egg
1 Tablespoon minced garlic
1/4 cup grated Parmesan cheese
1 Tablespoon butter, melted
2 Tablespoons sesame seeds

Grease a 9x13-inch baking pan. Dissolve yeast in warm water in mixing bowl. Add flour, oregano, shortening, sugar, salt, garlic powder, and egg. Beat on medium speed 2 minutes. Stir in minced garlic and cheese. Pat dough evenly in pan with floured hands. Let rise until doubled, about 20 minutes.

Cut dough into 3x1-inch sticks, in the pan. Brush with butter and sprinkle with seeds. Bake at 450 degrees for 12–15 minutes.

Makes 3 dozen breadsticks.

Ships serves these with almost any meal, and they're especially scrumptious dipped in clam chowder. Leftovers can be made into croutons.

# Chapter 12

*Neglect not the gift that is in thee . . .*
1 Timothy 4:14

The next morning Tanya delivered a nine-pound baby boy. Before our husbands went to work, we left them to watch our own kids, grabbed our wands and our auntie pins, and met in the hospital lobby.

"You girls have got to time these babies better," Maxine said, her eyes barely open. "I'm getting too old for these early hours."

We dashed to the nursery to see the baby, and I was relieved to hear she had named him Ryan, rather than Heathen. A nurse took him in to Tanya, and we all barged in after her.

"We're here," Maxine sang, as if Tanya must have been anxious for our arrival.

"You cannot believe what I went through this time," Tanya said. As we passed little Ryan around and clucked over his gorgeous olive complexion and his darling lips, Tanya detailed the entire labor and delivery, Preston's inability to coach "whatsoever," the doctor's surprise at the size of Ryan's head, and how she'd had to bark orders at everyone to get the job done right.

"I tell you, I will never do this again," Tanya said.

If doctors and nurses could vote on the matter, Tanya would probably have had her tubes tied that very minute. The nurses who popped in during our visit looked to be summoning strained patience with her.

"Hospitals should be like spas," Tanya said. "They should rub your feet and your back, they should bring you cool drinks, and they should play relaxing music."

"Pedicures, waxings," I said, pretending to go along with her wish list.

"Exactly," she said. "Then you go home looking better and feeling better. I mean, this is a huge ordeal! And don't get me started on the food."

"You are in a hospital," Crystal reminded her.

"Oh, there is no excuse for this kind of cooking," Tanya said, wagging her finger. "They need Marco in there to teach them a few Italian cooking tricks."

Ships chuckled. "Someone should start up a gourmet hospital, shouldn't they?"

We all agreed on this, then bestowed our fairy gifts upon Ryan. Maxine gave him "the best qualities of both parents," Crystal gave him "a bright mind," Ships gave him "unwavering faith," and I gave him "a sense of humor." With Tanya for a mother, he was going to need one.

Tanya looked at my pregnant stomach. "You want the room next door?" she asked.

"Hey, I'm ready," I said. "But I'm not due for another month."

Tanya gestured to little Ryan. "Well, you never know."

And I didn't. It turned out to be six more weeks before I delivered our first son, Dylan Matthew. I could hardly waddle, toward the end.

"Going overtime should only happen in ballgames," I told Jonathan. He agreed.

But every minute was worth it, as I looked into Dylan's face. I felt I had known him forever. He looked a lot like my dad's side of the family, and those familiar features seemed always to have been in my life. I wondered if we had been buddies in the pre-existence, and Jonathan and I decided we both had known him very well.

Little Hayley—who suddenly looked gigantic—couldn't wait to be the helpful big sister, patting him and saying "Diwwan.

Diwwan." She filled his bassinette with toys (the ones she no longer wanted, of course), and loved watching over him in his car seat as we drove along.

I knew it wouldn't last forever, so I soaked up and savored every minute of her adoration of her brother. She'd be a great mom one day, I decided.

Jonathan and I lavished them with all the love we could, taking them everywhere, thoroughly enjoying the world through their eyes. Everything was fresh and exciting—every bug, every flower was a new experience.

Eventually, I felt I could handle our luncheons again, with Hayley in a high chair, and Dylan gurgling happily in his carrier.

Crystal was amazing—she was juggling her three kids as if she'd done this all her life. And Ships's kids were older, of course. It was only Tanya who seemed to be overwhelmed and miserable again.

"How can you do it?" she shouted, dragging Molly and Ryan to our table. "I need a nanny. I truly do. What do you do if they both start screaming at the same time? What if you can't leave them alone even to take a shower? Help me, you guys!"

We settled in at the table, and Crystal patted Tanya's shoulder. "You'll get the hang of it," she said. "It's a lot easier than adjusting to the first one. I mean, that's scary—you wonder how to do it all. Now you have experience, you'll be fine."

Tanya's eyes rolled and she slumped dramatically. "I am not cut out for this," she said.

"Now, Tanya," I said, glancing pointedly at her kids, "Don't you think you should save those comments for other times?"

Tanya looked surprised. "Oh. Yeah!" Evidently it hadn't occurred to her not to complain about her children right in front of them.

"I've got to sit you down and have a talk," I whispered.

She rolled her eyes. "I know, I know."

"Of all people, *you* can certainly put on a happy face if you need to," Ships said.

Maxine clapped her hands. "Look how your talents are needed in motherhood!"

"That right!" I said. "Boy, we all need that one sometimes—when the car breaks down, the kids are sick, the power goes out—that's when we need Tanya's acting skills."

"No kidding," Ships said. "I'd love to be able to slap on a happy face whenever I need one."

Tanya smiled, almost shyly.

"Think of the difference it makes in the mood of the home," Crystal said, "when the wife is really trying to be calm and happy. I mean, it's a big difference."

We all acknowledged that this was true.

The waitress took our orders, and we all got the same pasta dish.

"We're becoming one another," Crystal said. "Chemistry, again."

"You know," Maxine said, "I think every single talent we're given can be used in mothering. I never got the chance, but think about it, girls. Every talent has application in the home."

And sure enough, we bandied about various talents—art, music, math, organizing, a great memory, dancing, sports—and decided every bit of it could enhance our family lives.

"I feel like I've had an 'aha' experience," Crystal said. "It's like conversational chemistry."

Ships grinned. "Yeah—we never realized how God made us to be mothers—we keep thinking we have to use whatever abilities we have somewhere else, or they're being wasted."

"Although I wonder about precision marching," Tanya teased.

Ships conked her on the head with a spoon. "We can march all over the house," she said, adding, "I always wanted a family that could march into church like the von Trapps. All well-behaved, all quiet." Ships's kids were adorable, but they were busy little explorers, often leading the other little kids in charges through the cultural hall.

"Oh, we all dream of perfect children," Crystal said. "I once vowed I would never bring Cheerios to church to keep my kids quiet. I'd train them early, and they'd just sit there obediently. Ha! We should buy *stock* in Cheerios."

I laughed. "It's true." Mine were so much younger, but already I could see that they had minds of their own. They weren't just obedient little wind-up toys. "You become a lot more tolerant of other parents."

"Oh my gosh, that is so true," Tanya said. "I never even say a word during Relief Society lessons anymore—the ones on parenting. I just sit back and let the younger sisters have all the answers."

"And didn't we?" I asked. "Boy, before I became a mother, I used to know exactly how parents ought to raise their children!"

"You get quieter and quieter, the older the kids get," Ships nodded.

"But you all have good children," Maxine said. We had a good laugh at that.

The pasta arrived and we all dug in, hungry. "Carbo loading like the athletes," Tanya said. Little did we know that in the years to come, carbs would be the bad guys.

Crystal twirled the pasta on her fork. "Oh, Christian has a Suzuki recital this Saturday—can you guys come?"

We had early on pledged to support each others' kids, and attend everything a relative would. We were each others' "unofficial" family—there to pick up the slack if our blood relatives bombed out (which often happened).

"I'm in," I said. All were able to make it, except Maxine, who had tickets to a matinee with some older sisters in the ward.

"I have to prepare for my calling," Tanya said, "but it shouldn't take that long. I just go in and share stuff in my pockets with the Primary kids."

"Oh—Sister Friendly!" I said. "I remember her. She would always come on the fifth Sunday and we loved it! She had all kinds of cool things to show us, all these neat object lessons that tied in with what we were learning . . ."

Tanya sighed. "Well, I just throw a bunch of stuff into my pockets and then tell 'em that's it. I stick the stuff back into my pockets and leave."

"You don't give anything to the kids?" Crystal asked.

"Nope."

We all groaned. "C'mon, Tanya, you have to make it fun."

"Be a sport."

"It's 'sharing time,' not 'selfish time,'" I scolded.

Tanya raised an eyebrow. "Really? Oh, I guess I read that wrong."

"Very funny," I said. "So basically you're Sister UNfriendly."

Tanya laughed. "I guess so."

"You're creative," Ships said, slapping her arm. "Do something cute with the kids."

Tanya sighed. "Okay, fine, fine. But if I have to go to the recital . . ."

"Oh, come on," Maxine said. "It's only Wednesday. And you've had all month to prepare!"

"Okay, okay, I'll do it!" Tanya shook her head. "There is no free agency in this group, have you noticed that?"

We laughed. "We're just helping each other succeed," Crystal shrugged.

* * *

The recital was in the basement of a church Crystal kept calling the Last Baptist Church. Folding chairs were arranged in semicircles and sugar-dusted shortbread cookies were on trays at the sides, for refreshments later. Crystal had brought the fruit slush.

A stout woman in a black evening gown stood up to introduce the musicians. We clapped wildly as little Christian took his place on a round wooden disc. He was holding a miniature violin. He bowed. Then he sat down.

"That's it?" I whispered to Ships. She shrugged.

We watched other kids play simple numbers, then the evening was over. At the punchbowl I caught up with Crystal, but wasn't sure what to say. "That was so . . . darling," I said.

"Thanks," she gushed. "He's still learning how to bow. You have to say 'hippopotamus' to yourself before you stand up."

"Of course you do," I said.

Crystal chuckled. "I know it seems funny, but this is the support these kids need. Then their confidence grows. Next time he'll be playing 'Twinkle, Twinkle.'"

"Oh, I can hardly wait," Ships whispered, as Crystal turned to talk with another parent.

"Don't you even think of inviting me to a concert like this for your kids," Tanya hissed into my ear.

I smiled, pretending to any onlookers that we were saying nice things about all their kids.

In the parking lot we agreed that if this was important to Crystal, we would support it. We might not understand it, but we would support it.

Just then, Crystal dashed out and said, "Oh, I'm so glad I caught you—I want you to come to Andrew's preschool graduation next Friday."

"Is it going to be like—" Tanya said.

"Of course we will!" I interrupted. Then I turned to the others. "And our kids would love to see that, so they can look forward to their own big days, won't they?" Ships and Tanya nodded. Crystal hurried back into the basement.

"A preschool graduation will be a lot better," Ships said to Tanya, to shush her.

"Let's get Maxine to come to that one," Tanya said. "Why should we suffer alone?"

But Maxine had a doctor appointment, so we had to go without her. It turned out to be far more elaborate than the concert. Every child wore a big cardboard flower around their heads, like a lion's mane. Andrew was a sunflower. Each one said something about growing bigger, and they sang a cute song about flowers growing in the garden, each one different, and so on.

I nudged Tanya. "See? This is cute."

"And now," the teacher said, "Andrew Wycomb has a poem."

"A poem he'd like to *read*," Crystal corrected.

"Yes. A poem to read," the teacher said.

Andrew walked up to the mike, stepped up on a little box, and smiled. Then he turned, buried his head in his shoulder, and blushed.

"Come on, Andrew," Crystal said. "You did it perfectly at home."

Still Andrew was scrunching.

"He's reading," Crystal said into the mike. "And I thought it might inspire the kids to see that."

I gulped. I could feel Ships looking over at me, but I didn't dare look back.

Finally Crystal read the poem herself, then said, "Just shy," to excuse Andrew's stage fright.

Afterward, we watched Crystal buzzing around the room, assuring all the other parents that Andrew really was reading already. "I know it's early, but he just picked it up so fast," Crystal kept saying.

"Uh, should we do something?" Ships asked.

"Oh, no," Tanya said, sarcastically. "Let's just let her brag about her superior child until she doesn't have a friend left in the room. Of course we should do something! Heather, you grab her."

"Me? Why should I be the one? You're the bravest, Tanya. You tell her."

Tanya sighed, then sashayed over to Crystal and pulled her away from a couple, saying, "Oh, I just have to steal her away for a minute." Then she whisked her over to our group, where none of us knew exactly what to say.

"You know we love you," I began.

"And we love Andrew," Tanya said.

"Uh-oh," Crystal said, putting her hands on her hips. "There's a BUT coming."

"But . . ." Ships said, "you're kind of . . . and not that we blame you—"

"No, not at all—he's a gifted boy, undoubtedly—"

"And we love that—"

"Yes, we're so proud of him—"

"But you're sort of . . . bragging," Tanya said, and winced.

Crystal's mouth dropped open. "I'm what?"

"Well, just a little," I said.

She released a burst of air in a little half-scream and leaned in. "You are jealous! I'm amazed at all of you. You are jealous of Andrew! I can't believe this!" Then she turned on her heel and huffed away.

"Well, that went well," I said. "Plan B?"

"Plan B is to let her find out the hard way, I guess," Ships said.

The next day I called her to apologize, but she was still on the offensive. "You're just like the T-ball mothers," she said. "It's amazing. Everywhere I go, moms are so competitive and jealous, they just can't stand to see someone who excels, or outshines their own child. I would think we would all be mature enough to handle that, but no."

"It's not that I'm not happy for Andrew," I said. "It's fantastic that he's reading. It's just—"

"It's just that yours aren't," Crystal retorted. And she hung up!

"That does it," I muttered, and dialed Ships. "Emergency meeting at my house," I said. "Bring Tanya."

"First of all," Tanya sneered, "her kids are older. Of course they're ahead."

"We can't take this personally," I said. "She has a problem. She must feel insecure or something, to need to do this. And she's evidently doing it at T-ball games as well."

Ships shook her head. "I'm no psychologist, but I think she's flipped her lid."

"What did she say to you?" Tanya asked. "I mean, your kids are waaay older."

"She just said I wouldn't know how to deal with a child who's working above his grade level."

We all groaned. "This is horrible," I said. "And it's not like Crystal. What has come over her?"

"Parenthood," Tanya said after a minute. "She's always been competitive, remember? She couldn't just make A's; she had to get the top A in the class."

"And now she's pushing her kids along ninety miles an hour," Ships said. "I'm not saying there aren't kids who want to read early, but Crystal is, like, determined that they will."

"Yeah, she's already worried about the SATs," I agreed. "But we can't just sit here and gossip—we have to help her. She won't have a friend left on a T-ball team or at PTA or anywhere."

"Maybe we should take her to lunch and tell it like it is."

"We kind of tried that at the graduation," I said. "It just made her madder."

"I know," Tanya said. "Let's tell her she's right. Her kid is superior and we were just feeling . . . I don't know . . . jealous. Maybe then she'll get down off her high horse and we can close the subject."

Ships and I both looked at her. "I think it's called *enabling?*" Ships said.

"And *lying?*" I added. "Plus, that won't solve the problem. We'll still be the only friends she will have. And it will probably start to affect her kids' social lives, too."

We all drummed our fingers on the breakfast bar and sipped our lemonade, thinking. "What's causing it?" I asked. "Why does she feel she has to impress everyone—or top everyone?"

"She sees life as a contest," Ships said. "She has to win."

"So we're all the enemy," I said. "The competitors she has to beat."

"Well, that's stupid," Tanya said. "I'm going over there right now and telling her we have it all figured out and that she better dang well get off it, 'cause she's wrecking the friendship."

Ships and I opened our mouths to argue with this, but then couldn't really think of a better idea. So we all hopped into my Volvo and drove to Crystal's.

She was showing flashcards to Ashley when we arrived, but invited us in nonetheless.

"So?" she asked, as if waiting for another apology.

"We, uh, we . . ." I stammered. "We should have brought Maxine."

"What does Maxine have to do with this?"

"Well, nothing, that's why we didn't involve her," Ships said. "She wasn't at the recital, or the graduation, so she wouldn't have seen it."

"Seen what?" Crystal's words slashed the air.

We all took a deep breath. Then Tanya went for it. "Crystal, you cannot point out to other people that their kids are stupid."

"It's just that . . . we want you to have friends and we're worried that you're kind of putting people off . . ." I said.

"Not that your kids aren't wonderful. It's just that . . . other people might sort of resent it being pointed out." Ships twirled a strand of her red hair around one finger.

Crystal stood up again, with her hands on her hips. "You make me sound like some kind of raving maniac, one of those pushy moms who—"

"Who tells everybody their kid is reading ahead of time, and who shoves them to the front for all the pictures, and who—" Tanya said.

"How can you say that?" Crystal shouted. "I am totally supportive of every child in that program! You're all just jealous. You can't stand to see my kids excel."

"No—we're proud of your kids," Tanya said.

"Then you'd be cheering them on instead of acting like it's so terrible to have bright children. Everyone is threatened by smart people. That is so backwards, and so sad—these kids should be celebrated, not hidden away!"

"You're right, they should," I interrupted. "But let us do it, instead of their mother. Then people won't see you as . . ."

Crystal shoved us all out the door and slammed it. We stood on the porch, bewildered.

"C'mon," I said, "let's just let her think about it. She'll talk to Peter. He's reasonable. He'll talk some sense into her."

We headed down the walkway, hoping Crystal would have an epiphany—the sooner the better.

It was two weeks before any of us even heard from Crystal. She sent each of us a note—including Maxine—asking us to meet her for lunch. I guess she didn't want to get into a conversation over the phone.

We met at a French crêpe place, and all of us were surprised when Crystal walked in wearing no makeup. She was always so perfect-looking that this really threw us. I guess we must have looked a little shocked.

"Just wanted to show you that I have given up being a perfectionist." She smiled. "I was really mad at you guys for a few days. But then I talked with Peter, and . . ." Now her eyes moistened. "I realized I have been a little over the top."

We all laughed and hugged her, glad to be a bunch of friends again. We had to explain the whole story to Maxine.

"Well, Crystal's children really are remarkable," Maxine said.

"But I need to let other people point that out," Crystal nodded, "like Heather told me."

"We'll be your public relations team," Tanya said. "I mean, you're already stuck with us coming to every event, so we'll do the bragging as well."

Crystal laughed. "Thank goodness you guys saved me before I alienated everyone I know. Looking back, I can't even remember what I was thinking. Can you believe I offered to let Andrew tutor another boy at T-ball? I thought his mother was so rude when she said, 'No, thanks,' but now I can see why. Peter pointed out that it puts a lot of pressure on the kids, too. They feel like they have to be the best or they'll disappoint me."

"Well, being a perfectionist has its ups and downs," I said. "I mean, your house is gorgeous—"

"But my kids have been really stressed out," Crystal said. "Being competitive is not always such a good thing. Although I do challenge each of you to come out to lunch without makeup next time."

"Oh, now she's gone too far," Ships said. "Did you forget I'm a redhead with white eyelashes? There is no way I'm stepping foot outside the house without mascara."

"You?" Maxine almost bellowed. "How about me? I'm *old*."

Crystal laughed. "If I can do it, you can all do it. Come on. Be good sports."

And so we did. The next month we showed up looking like we'd each just had an exfoliating facial.

"Okay," Tanya announced. "This was a great idea, Crystal. NOT. I will be the honest one. You people look like disaster victims, and we will not be doing this again."

We all agreed, and pulled out our makeup bags to put on at least some lipstick.

But then we voted that being imperfectionists was a good thing, and we decided we should relax the terribly high standards women often flog themselves with.

"We should all be like Sister Wettles," Tanya said, referring to a woman in our ward. "Bear your testimony about Miracle-Gro." We all laughed, remembering that awkward moment a few weeks ago, in a most imperfect testimony.

"Frankly, I wish you'd gain some weight and let yourself go a little bit," Tanya said to Crystal, who slapped her arm playfully. "You make the rest of us look bad. Stupid little size two pants."

"You're still almost the ideal LDS wife and mother," Maxine smiled, patting Crystal on the arm. "But it's like Bruce R. McConkie said, you don't have to be truer than true."

Ships brightened. "Maybe Maxine is finally rubbing off on us."

"We can only hope," I said.

# Mormon Slush

4 bananas
1 (12 -ounce) can frozen lemonade concentrate
1 (12 -ounce) can frozen orange juice concentrate
1 large (56 -ounce) can pineapple juice
1 1/3 cups sugar
6 cups water
1 1/2 large bottles 7-Up

In a large bowl, beat bananas with an electric mixer. Add frozen juice concentrates, pineapple juice, sugar, and water. Mix and pour into two 9x12-inch loaf pans. Freeze.

Remove from freezer 1 1/2 hours before needed, and let thaw. Place in punch bowl and mash all together with 7-Up.

Crystal likes to be the one who brings this, but if she isn't in your ward, you go ahead and get the compliments.

# Chapter 13

*And they shall also teach their children to pray, and to walk uprightly before the Lord.*

D&C 68:28

There are two kinds of children in the world: KKS (knick-knack safe) and KKH (knick-knacks hidden). If you do not remove breakable objects in a KKH's home, you will soon have KKSTS (knick-knacks smashed to smithereens).

People who say, "You just aren't firm enough—you need to say no and mean it," have KKS children, and simply don't realize it. KKS children can be persuaded not to touch things. Hayley, it turned out, was the founding member and official pace car of the KKH. She originated the "shake and break" school of exploration, which I'm thinking of putting on her resume someday. If an object cannot at first be broken into, a simple lob across the room will often do the trick, and then you can find out if, say, a globe is really hollow.

Hayley was grabbing sacks of beef jerky from a vertical clip bar in the supermarket when a woman asked me if she had ever been tested.

"No," I said, "but I have. Daily."

That night, I asked Jonathan if maybe we should have her tested.

"For what?" Jonathan asked. "Brilliance? She's a curious child, and very bright. It doesn't content her to sit in a cart and gum the handles, like a lot of kids. She wants to go and do and discover."

I nodded. Jonathan was probably right. Oh, maybe she wasn't a genius, but I knew she didn't have attention problems. When something caught her interest, she could focus on it for hours.

"Too many people are busybodies," Jonathan said. "You should have asked that woman if she'd been tested for *that*."

"Ah, good plan," I said. "You could write a book: *Daring New Missionary Techniques,* by Jonathan Bench."

He pulled me close and kissed me. "How about *Daring New Kissing Techniques?*"

"Oh, we'd better research that one some more." I smiled, and kissed him again.

Jonathan and I had been married for almost four years now, and couldn't have been happier. The kids were healthy, his business was going well, our families were fine, and orders for my dress designs were coming in regularly. We were even moving into a larger home, where the kids could each have their own bedrooms, and I could have a design studio. I remember asking a neighbor to take a photo of us in front of our old house, though, to save, the way President Bickmore did.

Of course the gang and their husbands showed up to help us haul boxes and unpack china. We always helped each other move. It was a ritual that Maxine enjoyed, because she got to cater it, rather than heft furniture. And she always brought her delicious macaroni and cheese, which the kids always gobbled up. Crystal and Peter had also moved into a larger home, and Tanya had moved a year before, in hopes of injecting some excitement into her marriage. She had decorated her new house in wild, splashy colors—a sharp contrast to the conventional almond-and-beige scheme of the eighties. I pictured Preston trying to shave in a purple bathroom with pink tile, and had to give the guy credit for being so easygoing.

So Tanya and Maxine and I were no longer in the same ward, and I was more grateful than ever that all of us made an effort to see each other fairly often.

It surprised me how much I enjoyed being a mother. I relished stroller walks, making clay for the kids, singing lullabies, combing their wet hair after a bath, teaching them to dress themselves, and watching their faces light up with delight every time they learned a new task.

The group of us started meeting in the park each week, as our kids romped and played together. Ships joined us on Saturdays, and her older kids pushed ours in their swings, or opened juice boxes for them. Crystal had four by this time, including newborn Joshua. Even Tanya seemed to love these times together, and became our official excursion planner. She came up with day trips all over northern California, from attending a production of *The Three Bears,* to visiting Daffodil Hill, to touring the Jelly Belly factory, to spending a weekend at the beach.

Our scrapbooks grew as we filled them with photos of birthday parties, trick-or-treating, and a traditional cookie day in early December, when all of us got covered with flour and sprinkles.

"We're a family," Crystal shrugged, as she changed Dylan's diaper one afternoon at the park. I had gone chasing Hayley across the soccer field, so Crystal just took care of matters for me. Molly was drinking from Christian's sippy cup, and Ryan was pushing Dylan's toy truck through the sand.

It seemed one of the kids was always having a birthday, so we fell into "the Insta-Party routine," as we called it. Tanya would bring the paper goods, balloons, and streamers; I'd show up with cupcakes; Ships would handle the party gifts and thank-you notes; and Crystal always brought punch and homemade ice cream. We loved each other's kids like our own, and loved being called "auntie" by them. Our husbands even got tagged with "uncle," and we gladly attended gymnastics meets, school plays, band recitals, and soccer games for anyone in the group.

We conferred with one another about toilet training, shoe tying, bed wetting, croup getting, and marble swallowing. We shared clothes, toys, books, and games. We dealt with lying, whining, tattling, and tantrums. Maxine always had advice from her years of observing other children—and the added benefit of being unbiased, of course. She usually came to the park with a basket full of Goldfish crackers, peanut butter sandwiches, and orange sections. Oh, yes, and wet wipes, a mother's number-one piece of equipment.

Eventually our kids went off to preschool and school, and except for Crystal's last two—girls named Sydney and Mallory— we found ourselves having lunch again without high chairs and infant carriers. Hayley was in second grade by this time, and looking forward to getting baptized on her eighth birthday. To me it seemed she was just learning to walk yesterday.

"Isn't it weird?" Ships said one day, sipping clam chowder at the wharf. "Between us, we have twelve kids!"

It was true—Crystal had six, and except for Maxine, the rest of us each had two.

"Who would have thought?" Tanya agreed. "I remember when we were still waiting to be asked out on a date! Where did the time go?"

"Wait until you're my age, honey," Maxine said, tearing off a piece of sourdough bread. "Christmas will roll around and you'll say, 'Wait—we just *had* Christmas!' And then your skin will dry out. I tell you, I feel like a walking loofah."

We all laughed, and compared age spots on our hands, and creases in our necks, to see if we were aging. Maxine just rolled her eyes.

"I wonder what we've all spent, collectively, on our kids," I said. "Think about it—summer camps, music lessons, sports—"

"Oh, you could each have a Mercedes, believe me," Maxine said. "And you could buy me one as well!"

"No fair," Tanya said. "I am definitely stopping at two, then, and starting a Mercedes fund." Tanya had ordered fried shrimp, and was passing the plate around for each of us to try one.

"And nobody start crying about turning thirty," Maxine said, "Or I'll smack you one."

We laughed. We were already complaining about how we looked in photos, and Maxine was always right there to remind us that one day we'd kill to look that good.

"Try this sauce," Tanya said. "It's a remoulade."

"Oh, yum, I love that stuff," Ships said, scooping some up with her shrimp.

"It's a wonder we don't all weigh five hundred pounds," Maxine said. "Who eats more than we do?"

We laughed. It was true; we loved life, we loved eating, and we loved one another.

We even vacationed together, usually meeting up in Yosemite or Carmel for a week during the summer. Our husbands also got along, though they stopped short of wiping one another's cheeks with a spitty thumb.

"I really enjoy these guys," Jonathan said one night when we were in our tent, after Hayley and Dylan had dozed off. "Peter is so solid, you know? He's smart, but he doesn't flaunt it. He has the humility of a General Authority."

It was true; I wouldn't have been a bit surprised if Crystal called one day to tell us they'd be moving to Salt Lake for a new calling of Peter's.

"And Preston is very quiet, but a super hard worker. He actually has a dry sense of humor once you get to know him. Pretty quick on his feet."

"Preston gets overshadowed by his flashy wife," I agreed.

"And Marco is a riot. He's always up for a great gag, loves to go golfing, sings opera at the top of his lungs. He should have his own TV show."

"His own Italian cooking show," I agreed.

"But I think I would have liked Sam the very best," Jonathan said. He was still trying to make our marriage exactly like Maxine's had been.

"He would have liked you, too, I'll bet."

Jonathan turned onto his side and kissed me. "I want the best marriage in the world," he whispered.

"Well," I whispered back, "I've already got it. But I'll share."

Jonathan smiled, then ran his fingers through my hair. "You have moonlight all over you," he said.

"You have stars in your eyes," I whispered back.

We kissed, then kissed again.

"The kids are going to think we're really corny one day," I said.

Jonathan shrugged. "The kids will be lucky to have a relationship half this good."

Just then Tanya ripped open the flap of our tent and hissed, "Are you guys still up?"

I closed my eyes and smiled, relieved that a little kissing was all she had interrupted.

"We're up," Jonathan sighed.

"Good. Because there's a bear tearing into your trunk."

"What?" Jonathan leaped to his feet and scrambled out of the tent. Thank goodness we had decided to sleep in our clothes.

"Get back here!" I shouted. "Stay away from him."

But Jonathan was gone, with Tanya following right behind. "Don't run up to a bear!" I screamed, slipping into my loafers and taking off after them.

Crystal was already in Pioneer Woman mode, gathering the children into her tent and telling them everything would be all right. Of course, the only experience any of our kids had with bears was hearing about the three who met Goldilocks, or the Berensteins who lived in a tree with curtains at the windows, so they were all thinking, *Well, of course it will be all right.*

Marco, Preston, and Peter were all waving huge sticks, and yelling at a bear who had grabbed something out of our trunk and had lumbered off into the woods, his fur rippling as he ran. The men came walking back to the campsite revved up like cavemen who had just scared off a saber-toothed tiger.

Maxine and Ships were just joining the fray, tying their bathrobes and wiggling into flip-flops. "What happened?" Maxine asked.

"Oh, just a little bear," Marco said. "But we scared him away."

"It wasn't that little," Jonathan said.

"It was a giant grizzly," Preston added, shaking his stick. "But we protected the womenfolk and children."

We all went over to our car, to see what damage had been done. The bear had apparently smelled a package of bacon inside, and had rocked the car until the trunk had popped open, then pawed through our camping gear. Just as the men had come running, he had found his prize and taken off with it through the trees.

"You're all lucky he didn't attack you," I said. "I can't believe you went running up to a bear. Especially when food was around."

"I agree," Maxine said. "That was mighty foolish."

"What was foolish was packing bacon," Jonathan said, giving me a glance.

Two minutes ago I had been bathed in lavender moonlight, and now I was to blame for a bear in the camp.

"The brochures all said if it was locked away it would be safe," I said, in defense of my judgment.

"That's true," Tanya said. "But I still wouldn't have brought bacon."

We took out the rest of the food, then tied the bent trunk lid closed with a piece of rope. The kids were all disappointed that they hadn't gotten to see the bear, and Andrew (almost eleven) was saying we should pray for it to come back. Crystal was wondering if we should pack up and leave.

"They're supposed to leave the campers pretty much alone," I said.

"And dogs are supposed to scare away burglars," Ships said. She had recently been robbed, despite owning a big Doberman pinscher.

"Okay, let's find a motel," Jonathan said.

The kids began to groan that they'd never get to see a bear, and we weren't any fun.

"This is why children don't get to go camping alone," Peter said. Then he promised we'd look for a place with a swimming pool, so the kids quickly forgot about the bear as they anticipated doing cannonballs into a heated pool.

Our other joint vacations were a little less eventful, though we managed to accumulate our share of stories that the kids told and retold over the years. There was a haunted elevator that made creepy sounds in a ghost town we visited. We saw a family of hawks in a nest below a cliff where we were hiking. We attended general conference in Salt Lake together. We went boating on Lake Powell. We explored the Oregon coastline.

And on Sundays we always made sure to find a ward building, or hold a sacrament meeting of our own around a campfire. Years later, it was the shared spiritual moments that were what our children loved recalling the best.

The kids grew lanky and tan, baby teeth giving way to permanent teeth, and fuzz growing on their legs. We bought each other's candy and magazines for school fund raisers, cheered on whatever kid was in a school play, and attended each others' hamster funerals. We passed on baseball uniforms, karate jackets, dancing leotards, and piano books. We had created our own mini-village.

"So tell us how teenagers are," I said to Ships during one luncheon. Gino had just turned thirteen. "What can we expect?"

"Well," she said, thinking. "You can save money on umbrellas, because you cannot get a teenager to carry one."

"Oh, right," Tanya said. "It isn't cool enough."

"No, they'd rather catch pneumonia," Ships said. "They're always worrying about what their friends think, instead of what you think."

We all grimaced. *No! They can't forget us! We gave birth to them! We love them! How can some greasy-haired kid be more important than us?*

"I am dreading that," Crystal said. "I know it happens, but I don't even want to think about it."

"Well, brace yourselves," Ships said. "Even Francesca is thinking more about clothes and popularity this year. You want to shield them from the world."

"Thank goodness for the Young Women's program," Tanya said. "That'll save the day."

"Are you kidding?" Ships laughed. "O ye of little brains. The Church programs are just a supplement. Don't forget that. The main training has to be in the home. And let me tell you, it's not always easy."

Crystal was giving Ships a funny look.

"I've seen that look before," I said. "That's the 'maybe your kids, but not my kids' look."

Crystal smiled, caught. "Well, I just can't believe that my kids will succumb to all that."

Maxine laughed. "Oh, Crystal, you are so entertaining. Every child is somewhat a product of the time when they grew up. You can have your influence, but you can't control what goes on outside your house."

"It's horrible," Ships agreed. "You wait."

"Oh, thanks a lot," I said. "Now we're all scared to death."

"Well, you should be," Ships laughed. "These kids are exposed to stuff we never even heard of. Plus all the split families, day-care fallout, the media—"

"Shall I tell you what I've observed?" Maxine said. She always couches her advice this way, to let us know that she's well aware she is speaking without actual experience. "If you can help your child gain a testimony, then even when you can't be there, the Holy Ghost can be."

We all sat in silence for a while, mesmerized by this powerful thought. It was the most comforting parenting tip I'd heard in a long time. First, testimony. Then, that child is fortified against many of the temptations life offers up. Like our Church leaders always tell us, you need to live a Christ-centered life to protect yourself.

Suddenly all the extra stuff didn't seem important. So what if you don't sign up for baseball one season? Or if you pass on violin and flute camp? The larger goal takes precedence. Each of us committed to inject more spirituality into our extracurricular time, instead of so many distractions. We all went home with renewed optimism for raising our kids in this day and age.

* * *

When Dylan was two and a half, we signed him up for a Mommy-and-Me play group, two mornings a week. We had done the same with Hayley, and she had loved it. There were new songs to learn, new stories to hear, and new kids to meet.

The first day, we started with giant beach balls, rolling them back and forth, then went over to the wooden puzzles, and sat down with an easy puzzle of shapes. Two other kids were whipping through them, and going on to tougher puzzles of ships and trains. Dylan twirled the stem of an orange triangle piece in his chubby little fingers, then tried to fit it into the circle spot. Over and over, he tried to press it in. Finally he tried to put it in the rectangle spot. Gently I guided his hand to the triangle, and the piece plunked into place.

When we all formed a circle for singing and clapping time, Dylan stretched out over my lap and fiddled with his shirt buttons. When they passed out instruments, the other kids all used them to make sounds, but Dylan just sucked on the wooden sticks he was given.

An obstacle course was worse—Dylan stepped over the tubes he was supposed to crawl through, and went to look out the window before finishing the course. Kids helped with cleanup, putting balls in a giant garbage can. Dylan picked one up to help, but then dropped it beside the can, instead of putting it inside.

As I buckled him into the car, I was worried. I wanted to say, "This stupid school is too pushy—they want kids to master the skills of a seven-year-old!" But in my heart, I wondered if something was wrong with Dylan.

That night, Jonathan listened as I explained what I had seen. "It wasn't until he was grouped with kids his own age that I could see how far behind he is," I said.

"Well, it was only the first day, honey. I don't think you should worry so much. Why don't you see how he does the rest of this week, and next week? I'm sure he'll get used to it, and participate more. You'll see."

I had my misgivings, but I smiled and agreed as he kissed the top of my head.

But Dylan didn't get "used to it." If anything, he began to pay less attention to the games and activities. He didn't seem bored, but he just didn't seem to care about doing anything other than playing with balls and toys.

I waited three weeks before talking to Jonathan about it again. The ladies at the school were nice, but I could tell they were thinking Dylan was slower than the other kids. The last straw for me was one day when we went back to the puzzles we had worked on that first day. Dylan picked up a blue square and waved it around. He then tried it in a couple of spots, but not the square spot. After a while, he lost interest in that, and began sliding the square around on the carpet like it was a car. I wondered why Dylan hadn't made any progress at all—it was the same puzzle, for crying out loud! I blinked back tears as we drove home.

Jonathan agreed that we should get a medical evaluation. Our pediatrician referred us to some developmental experts, and they put Dylan through a series of tests not unlike the preschool toys. "Point to the book," they said, holding up a card depicting a duck and a book. Dylan just looked around the room, got up, and went to bang on a xylophone.

"Where is the dog?" he was asked. Three cards were on the table, showing a dog, a tree, and a house. Dylan just banged his fists on the table, happily making drum sounds. He didn't pass even one of their tests.

I knew the results would be hard to take, especially when the testers kept staring into their laps, instead of looking up at us when they came to give us the bad news.

Finally, one of them said, "Dylan has some developmental delay."

"What does that mean?" I asked. "Is he mentally retarded?"

"No, no," the other one assured me. "He is just a bit slower than average."

The first one glanced at the other, then said, "A good deal slower. We would recommend that you place him in a class for children with special needs."

"What—for his whole life?" Jonathan asked.

"Well, who can tell?" the second tester said, trying to soft-pedal it again. "We'll just have to evaluate him periodically and see where he stands."

"What caused this?" I asked.

"It just happens sometimes," I was told. "It's not inherited; it's not anything you ate or did when you were pregnant; it's just the way Dylan was born."

"Well, can't he be in a normal class and just have extra help so he can keep up?"

They shook their heads. "It doesn't work that way. He can't learn at the same rate as the other children. It would probably frustrate him as well."

Jonathan and I looked at our little punkin', then at one another. I fought the urge to cry, and Jonathan pulled me close. Suddenly I remembered the impression I had received in the temple. I had felt that I was to bear a unique child. But this was not what I had expected.

That evening we talked about all the possibilities. "Maybe he'll outgrow it," I said. "That could happen. I know—priesthood blessing! That's what he needs."

Jonathan did bless him, but both of us suspected this would be Dylan's cross to bear in life, and that we, as a family, would simply have to adapt to his abilities. He was such a lovable, good-natured baby. I could only pray that Heavenly Father would help him live a normal life and be able to marry one day. It was a prayer that rarely left my lips.

We looked into every special education program available. We talked with other parents in a support group. We explained it to our families, who were wonderfully supportive. And finally, we realized that Dylan was a blessing to us. He might not have the intellectual capabilities of other boys, but he was doubly endowed with a sweet personality, a natural tendency to obey, a joyous heart, the determination to try again, and a thousand other traits that would help him through life. Had we signed up for a special-needs child in the pre-existence? Who knew—but it didn't matter. Here he was, we loved him to pieces, and we would give him the happiest life we could. I had been prepared for this child in the temple. He may have been slower intellectually, but he was a magnificent spirit who would enrich our lives and bless us eternally.

"You'll probably have fewer worries than other families," Maxine said at one lunch, when everyone was trying to cheer me up. "He'll probably never rebel or put you through worries about drugs, or sex—seriously, think about that. Here is a precious little child of God, who will always be an absolute sweetheart."

I smiled. It seemed true of other families I had known that had children with handicaps. They seemed made of softer, more spiritual material.

"No reason he can't have a strong testimony," Ships said. "And even serve a mission. There are lots of ways he can do that."

"Absolutely," Tanya said. "And he'll be able to live independently one day. I mean, people with real retardation can do it, Heather. You know Dylan will be okay."

"And he's in the regular preschool right now, learning social skills and making friends," Ships said. "He's probably the happiest one there."

"It's true," I said. "He loves going there. I don't think anyone notices a difference, yet."

"Wouldn't life be grand if we never noticed differences?" Maxine said. "No comparisons—just acceptance."

When I looked at Crystal, I noticed big tears rolling down her cheeks. She caught her breath in chatters. "I am so sorry, Heather," she said.

"What for?"

"I am such a jerk." Crystal wiped her eyes with her napkin. "I can't believe I said you were jealous because Andrew was reading early. I feel like the worst friend." She sobbed into her hands. "Please forgive me."

I started crying, too, and Ships slung her arm across my shoulders. "Dylan will learn to read," she whispered. "He will."

"But it doesn't matter," Crystal said, still crying. "It is so stupid and unimportant! I am so sorry—what matters is his testimony, like Maxine told us. I will never compare anyone's kids to mine again. This has really taught me a lesson."

"It's okay," I said, when the tears slowed down. "We all want our kids to do well."

Crystal shoved her lunch away. "I can't eat this. Anybody want some?"

Nobody did.

"You didn't know," I said, again trying to comfort Crystal.

"What do you bet every one of your kids turns out better than mine?" she said, addressing all of us. "That would really show me, huh?"

"Now, girls," Maxine said, dabbing Crystal's eyes with a handkerchief from her purse. "The Savior loves us all the same. He doesn't care who learns to read first," and she looked at me, "or last. We just need to support each other, and help when help is needed."

Crystal hugged her. "You're right, Maxine. I love you, Heather. And I love little Dylan—" She started crying again. "Please forget what I said."

I reached across Tanya to pat her hand. "It's forgotten."

"He's our boy," Tanya said. "I mean, we're his aunties, and we'll all help in any way we can."

The others chimed their agreement, and I sat with my napkin pressed to my cheeks, catching tears of joy.

# Remoulade Sauce
### (Wonderful with shrimp or with crab cakes)

2 Tablespoons vinegar
2 Tablespoons Dijon mustard
2 Tablespoons ketchup
2 teaspoons tarragon
2 teaspoons paprika
2 cloves garlic, minced
1/2 teaspoon black pepper
1/4 teaspoon kosher salt
1/4 teaspoon hot pepper sauce
2/3 cup olive oil
1 cup green onion, chopped
1 Tablespoon flat-leaf Italian parsley, chopped
2 lemons, thinly sliced

Maxine says this recipe is too much trouble, and just uses Thousand Island dressing or tartar sauce. But that is not the same—not by a long shot. Try it my way, and you'll agree it's worth it.

Combine vinegar, mustard, ketchup, tarragon, paprika, garlic, black pepper, kosher salt, and hot pepper sauce in a blender or food processor. Whirl until puréed. With motor running, slowly drizzle in oil in steady stream to emulsify. Pour into bowl. Stir in green onions and parsley. Serve with shrimp, garnish with lemon slices. Keep chilled.

Serves 6.

# Chapter 14

*For all have not every gift given unto them; for there are many gifts, and to every man is given a gift by the Spirit of God. To some is given one, and to some is given another, that all may be profited thereby.*

D&C 46:11–12

Dylan was the greatest thing ever to happen to our family. His pure affection, his sincere love, his eagerness to laugh—Jonathan and I decided our family was blessed beyond our wildest wishes when Dylan was born. He was a constant example of how we really need to be—childlike, faithful, generous, kind. Whenever one of us would get cross or impatient, self-pitying or proud, there was Dylan to bring us back into line.

Hayley adored him. Her quick mind and natural athletic ability made her shine, but she remained humble and grateful for her blessings, because of Dylan. She also remembered to keep her gifts in perspective, and realize that gifts of the Spirit are the choicest ones. She had an extra tender heart for the kids at school with disabilities, too, and came swiftly to their defense if ever they were being persecuted or overlooked.

As Dylan grew and learned new skills, it was Hayley who led the applause for him. It was ten times tougher for Dylan to learn how to ride a bike than it was for other kids, and when he finally did it, we celebrated big time. We threw a bicycle party, inviting all the neighborhood kids to the park, where Dylan led them in a bike parade. Then we enjoyed a bike-shaped cake, punch in take-home water bottles, and awards for best-decorated bike, shiniest bike, coolest helmet, loudest bike horn, and softest seat! Dylan's accomplishments made us slow down, smell the roses, and appreciate every step forward.

The girls were wonderful with Dylan—each of them took him on a special excursion with their own families, once a year. You couldn't have convinced him that these dear friends were not real aunties. They were his world and he loved them fiercely.

At lunch one day I presented each of them with a gift Dylan had made them. He had made clay pinch pots, and then had them glazed and fired in a kiln at school. Painstakingly, he had written each of their names inside the bowls.

"I will treasure this just as much as anything my kids ever made," Crystal said, tracing the rim with a finger. "This pot is full of Dylan's love."

Ships began crying. "He is so wonderful," she said. "He just gives things spontaneously to others. I have to threaten my kids with grounding just to get them to write thank-you notes."

"Well, no kid likes doing that," I said. I took a bite of my chicken salad.

"But he is the most generous guy," Tanya said. "I love this pot! Look—he remembered that I like purple."

Maxine's was the biggest, but she graciously didn't point that out. "I love mine, too," she said. "It's going right on the dining table."

"You've all been so great with him," I said. "We'll never be able to thank you enough for making him feel so loved."

"That kid is going to the celestial kingdom," Ships said. "I hope you all know that." She popped a forkful of poached salmon into her mouth.

"Now it's up to us to get there as well," Maxine agreed, "so we can all be with him."

"Oh, I want us all to be together there," I said. "I wish we could be sealed or something."

"We'll probably be neighbors," Crystal said. "At least, I hope so."

Tanya shrugged. "You guys can come and visit me in a lower kingdom. I doubt I'm going where you're going."

We all had to scold her and assure her that the Celestial Kingdom was certainly within her reach.

"Even if I get a divorce?"

We all stopped, mid-chew. Tanya's tone was not laced with her usual kidding or sarcasm.

"Are you serious?" Crystal asked.

"Looks like it," Tanya sighed.

Now we all blustered, "What?" "You can't do this!" "Can't you try another counselor?" "Are you sure this is for the best?"

But Tanya was immovable. "It's impossible," she said. "Preston's the one filing. He thinks I'm a terrible mother, which is probably true . . ."

We all jumped in again to assure her that was wrong.

"And," she said, "my going out of town so much on acting calls has made him feel abandoned. The kids, too, I guess."

"There must be something that can save the marriage," Maxine said. "For the sake of the kids?"

Tanya shook her head. "I told him I'd quit acting completely, but he said I've made that promise too many times."

I thought back to our talk when Tanya first learned she was pregnant with Ryan. Since then she had sworn off acting several more times. I wondered why she couldn't have done it in moderation—just a play now and then, or an occasional audition. She was probably down in Los Angeles as much as she was home, and her absence had already taken a toll on the kids. Both of them were getting into trouble at school, and hanging out with a fast crowd. It broke my heart to see little Molly, now almost a teenager, dressing and acting like a pop star. We had each taken her to lunch to try to reason with her, but it hadn't seemed to make any difference. She was headstrong like her mother.

"I doubt the kids will even notice," Tanya said, laughing bitterly. "I'm gone half the time anyway."

"Oh, Tanya," I said. "You can't let this happen."

"Well, it's too late, I'm afraid," she said, leaning in to whisper, "Preston has found someone else."

"What?!" We were flabbergasted. "When? Who? How?"

"He's moving out next week," Tanya said. "Into an apartment in the same complex as this girl from work. At least it will be in a different ward."

Then she told us how Preston had fallen in love with a girl in her twenties, who idolized him. "I doubt he could find someone in their thirties who'd idolize him," Tanya snapped. "We're old enough to see a man as he really is."

I stared at my lap, and—thankfully—didn't say that I still idolized Jonathan. I just left her comment there on the table to get cold. Clearly she had no affection or admiration for Preston, and he had apparently sought out someone else who did.

"Oh, Tanya, my heart is aching," Maxine said. "I want you to be happy. I was so sure you and Preston could . . ."

Tanya swirled the ice cubes in her glass. "We talked to the bishop," she said. "He wanted us to try again, but now that Preston's in love with someone else, that's pretty unlikely."

"He should have waited until you were divorced," Ships said.

"No kidding," Tanya said.

We all sat in silence, taking in the horrible news and wishing we knew something comforting to say.

Finally Crystal spoke up. "Okay, Preston may have made his choice, but his free agency doesn't have to keep you out of the celestial kingdom. You can move right on without him."

"Yes," Maxine agreed. "You just draw close to Christ, and do everything you can to live worthy of your temple blessings . . ."

Now we all chimed in to assure Tanya that her divorce did not have to end her spiritual progress.

None of it seemed to lift her spirits, but she did thank us for trying. "I just have to get through this," she said.

And all we could do was offer to be there.

"I have to say that I kind of blame Tanya," I whispered in bed to Jonathan one night, not even sure if he was still awake.

He turned over to face me. "Tanya has never taken the teachings of the prophets very seriously," he whispered back.

"I know," I said, my eyes welling with tears. "And now look what's happened."

"When you have kids you have to make choices."

"And sacrifices," I agreed. "Now she has nothing." I wept for my friend. I felt she could have made the marriage work and I was a little angry that she hadn't kept trying. But she was still my friend, and even in her mistakes, I wanted to be there for her, and love her. I tried to remember that it wasn't my place to judge her—only to love her. Something told me she'd realize her errors one day, and even though it might be too late to reconstruct her family, she could still repent and find her way. I knew she had a testimony; she just needed to make hard choices and stick with them. The best help I could give would be to stay her friend through the process.

\* \* \*

The divorce proceedings were amicable, considering Tanya's volatile personality and Preston's insistence on bringing his new girlfriend, Noleen, to many of the meetings.

"Naturally, I slice her to ribbons," Tanya said, when we met for a fast brunch one morning. "I ask her if she brought any homework along, if they're going to honeymoon at Chuck E. Cheese's, that sort of thing."

"Which she no doubt appreciates," I said.

"You know," Maxine said, stabbing the air with her fork to punctuate her thoughts, "that woman is going to have some influence on your children—maybe you should try to get along with her."

"Hey, that's an acting job even I would turn down."

Crystal lifted the top of her omelet and blew steam away. "Still, you don't want to be enemies."

"Hey, she chose to be my enemy by dating my husband!" Tanya snapped. "She's trying to steal both him and my kids! They want full custody—can you believe that?"

We all commiserated with her and Tanya calmed down. "I ought to give it to them," she said. "That would serve them right. Molly and Ryan are not the easiest kids to raise, you know."

As it turned out, Tanya and Preston shared custody and came to a workable compromise on splitting up the property. Two weeks after the divorce was final, Preston wed Noleen, and Tanya had a bonfire at the beach, burning her wedding album and all her other pictures of Preston.

We agreed to come, even though it was cold and windy, because Tanya insisted this would bring her "closure." We were in our mid-thirties at this point, and closure was a big thing in the brand-new nineties.

Maxine actually brought marshmallows and skewers, so we sat in a circle around the fire and toasted them.

"Why do I feel like a druid?" I said.

"It does seem weird to be toasting marshmallows over Preston's remains," Crystal said.

"They're not his remains," Tanya said, rolling her eyes.

"Well, it seems like it," Crystal said.

"Hey, I'm not saying that wouldn't be fitting," Tanya said.

We all booed and ohhed to let her know she had gone over the line, but wishing her ex-husband dead was evidently part of her closure, because after our beach ordeal, she really seemed to accept the situation and mellow out about it. Even her comments about Noleen wound down, and she adapted to the schedule of Molly and Ryan going back and forth.

Unfortunately, in the ensuing years, Molly and Ryan took a nosedive. Within the same month in 1996, Molly tested positive for drugs, and Ryan was pulled over for drunk driving. The police found stolen goods in his trunk, and he was only sixteen, so they added underage drinking to the charges.

"Emergency luncheon," Maxine said, calling us to a new French restaurant not far from Golden Gate Park.

Ships arrived in a huff, after arguing with her dry cleaner. "How can they make you sign a release that if they ruin your clothes, you won't sue?" she started in. "What if restaurants tried to do that? You sign a release that if their food makes you sick you won't sue? What kind of world is this turning into?"

Maxine pulled her down into the booth, then whispered, "I told Tanya to meet a half hour later than I told the rest of you, so we could talk first—you know, decide what we can do . . ."

"About what?" Ships asked.

Maxine told her the trouble Molly and Ryan were in, and Ships groaned. "Oh, geez—Francesca having a messy room suddenly seems like nothing."

"We need to come up with some real help," Maxine said.

Crystal shook her head. "I have no idea. Stick them in a lock-down school where they can't do that stuff?"

"I'll bet that costs a fortune," Ships said.

"Maybe we could all chip in," I suggested.

"Maybe," Maxine said. "Or get Molly into a rehab place?"

"How about we have an intervention?" Ships said. "We sit them both down, and we have our husbands there, and we tell them how much we love them, and—I don't know—what do they do at interventions?"

"We definitely don't want Tanya or Preston to feel like we're putting the blame on them," Maxine said. "It's probably hard enough for them to see what's happening."

"To be honest," I said, "I put a little blame on myself. I wish I had been a better aunt. Maybe I could have done something—"

"Oh, no, you don't," Ships said. "You are not blaming yourself for this. You—we all—took those kids under our wings, and helped all we could. We even went to their open house nights at their schools."

"I know," I said, my mind flicking over images of Molly and Hayley making cookies together, Molly and the kids getting splashed at Sea World, Molly clapping for Dylan when he rode his bike. I thought of Ryan camping out with all the dads, Ryan playing a pirate in a school play and all of us giving him a standing ovation. What had happened?

"I'll tell you what happened," Maxine said, as if reading my mind. "Free agency happened. You can do everything right, exactly by the book, and your kids can still make wrong choices. Look at Heavenly Father—look how many he lost to Satan."

We all nodded. "And the divorce didn't help," Crystal said.

"No," Maxine agreed, "but this could have happened even if they'd stayed together."

"No one knows," I said.

"And," Ships pointed out, "they could still turn around. Maybe they'll be giving talks one day, telling how wild they were in their teens."

Crystal nodded. "It's never over until it's over."

Tanya breezed through the front door just then, and we waved her over.

"Well, this looks like the committee to choose Mother of the Year," she said, pretending enthusiasm. "Look no further, because here I am!"

"Oh, come on now," Ships said. "You can't judge your mothering by what your kids do."

"No?" Tanya asked, slipping out of her jacket. "Look at what's happening! I should have never married, and just been an actress in the first place, with no other attempts to do anything else."

"That's not true," Crystal said. "Heavenly Father knows how hard we each try, and you can be a wonderful mother and still have . . . this . . . happen."

"It could be a lot worse," Maxine said.

"Yeah, you're right," Tanya sneered. "They could be in jail. Oh, wait—they *are* in jail." Then she told us how Ryan was hauled off for having stolen electronics equipment, and Molly was right behind him, strung out on meth.

"Molly could be pregnant," Maxine said, trying to think of something worse.

"Yes, you are right," Tanya said. "It could be one tiny bit worse. Molly could be pregnant."

"I guess this doesn't help you feel much better," Maxine said, resting her hand on Tanya's.

"So what are you planning to do?" I asked. "We want to help."

"I'm planning to run away to Europe," Tanya said. "I guess you could help me pack."

"I could teach you Italian," Ships said, playing along.

"You can use my frequent flyer miles," Maxine said. "Ever since I hit sixty-five, flying hurts my ears."

"What about Singapore?" Tanya said to Maxine. "You were always going to go there."

"Well, then, I'll have to swim or take a boat," Maxine laughed.

"You should definitely get to Singapore," Tanya said.

"Back to the subject of our luncheon," Crystal sang, clearing her throat. "We really want to know what we can do."

"Let's order, first," Tanya said. "I'm having the crab-and-mushroom crêpes."

"Lamb chops for me," Maxine said.

We all ordered, then Tanya said, "There's not a thing any one of you can do. I talked with Preston, and we can't afford a dry-out for Molly. Ryan just probably needs to face the consequences and do some time, unfortunately."

I gulped and thought about how, fifteen years ago, we had been sitting around like this talking about diapers and bottles. Then it was action figures and dolls. Then it was science projects and spelling bees. And now, suddenly, we were talking handcuffs and mug shots.

"Maybe he can learn a skill in jail," Crystal said. Ryan hadn't done very well in school.

"Yeah, like breaking and entering," Tanya chirped. "Or how to use various guns and weapons."

"We can't let him go to jail," Maxine said. "He could come out some kind of criminal."

"He's already some kind of criminal," Tanya said. "He was selling stolen equipment for somebody. How come I'm the only one who can really face the reality here?"

We all stammered, and finally I blurted, "But he's our boy, too. It can't be happening."

"Okay," Tanya said, "you're where I was when I first got the call. Disbelief. But then you move on to Hurt, then to Furious, then to where I am right now, which is Cynical."

Crystal frowned. "What comes after Cynical?"

"Resigned and Depressed," Tanya said, "which is closing in on me."

"What about taking some kind of positive action?" I said. "That's got to help you feel better."

"Good idea," Tanya said, sarcastically. "I should go around to the schools and give assemblies about how not to trash your life before you're even out of acne cream."

"I mean, let's get Molly some help."

"Do you have any idea what that costs?"

"But if we all pitch in together," I said, "I'll bet we could do it."

Crystal nodded. "We could get her into rehab."

"We want to do this," Maxine said.

Tanya just stared at us. "But . . . you've got your own kids . . . and braces, and college . . .'"

"But your kids are our kids, too," Ships said. "We can't just sit by and do nothing, Tanya."

Tanya sighed and leaned her head back, staring at the ceiling. When she looked back at us her eyes were filled with tears. "I can't believe I have friends who would volunteer to do that." She grabbed us each in a tight hug. "I don't deserve this," she said. "You guys are angels. I swear, absolute angels."

We had a meeting with our husbands, and came up with a figure that would help the Towers make the payment, and Molly was pulled from school and put into a rehab program not far away.

Tanya was overjoyed. "For the first time ever, I feel some hope," she said. "And Molly is totally stunned that you would help her. I think it's the first time she's realized that she's somebody. You know? She's not just another statistic, but a person people can love."

Ryan did indeed serve some jail time, and the aunties showed up for visiting twice. Once to tell him off and remind him of how much we had cared for him and what a rotten way this was to repay women who had changed his very diapers. Then we realized the guilt tactic might not have been the best approach, so we came back with our wands, and reminded him of his birth gifts.

"We love you," I said. "You could have been sent to any one of us, and I don't think we could love you more."

"That's right," Ships said. "So you have to get your life in order, or you mess up our pact."

Ryan twisted in his chair behind the glass partition, and smiled. "What pact?"

"Are you kidding?" Ships shouted. "The pact to help each other and all our kids succeed."

"Guess I messed you up pretty good," Ryan said.

Ships stood up to chew him out again, but Maxine pulled her back down into her chair.

"There isn't a day that goes by that we don't pray for you," I said, beginning to cry. "If you ever wonder who loves you in this world, you remember your aunties."

Crystal jumped up. "And the minute you get out, we want to help get you into a vocational school, and get you away from those crummy friends who got you in here." She was waving her wand like a whip.

Maxine shushed her, whispering, "This was going to be a friendly visit . . ."

Ryan stared at us, then smiled and shook his head. "Thanks," he said.

"You'd better appreciate this," Maxine said at last, forgetting her own advice. "These are busy women with families to take care of. And they're pledging their support to you."

Ryan laughed. "I do, I do."

"All right, then," Maxine said, rising to leave. And then, ominously, "We'll be watching."

Ryan laughed again and waved good-bye as we slipped out and down the hallway.

"I wonder if there's a visitor's etiquette book," Crystal said as we headed to the parking lot.

"If so, I'm sure we just broke every rule," I said. "But I thought Maxine's threats were a nice touch."

"Well, that boy needs to straighten up," Maxine said. "Jail! The very idea."

\* \* \*

At our next luncheon Tanya had a meltdown. We had all been talking normally, when she suddenly started wheezing.

"Have you got asthma, girl?" Maxine asked, half-rising. She looked ready to dash from the restaurant to the hospital.

Tanya shook her head, trying to control her breathing. "I think the weight of this whole thing has finally . . ."

What whole thing? The rest of us looked at each other. None of us could figure out what she was talking about. As far as we knew, things seemed to be going as well as could be expected.

"What are you talking about?" Ships asked.

"My divorce," Tanya said. Now tears were rolling down her cheeks and she seemed to struggle for each breath. "It has settled on my own shoulders," she whispered. "I caused it. Every bit of it."

We listened as she took us through her entire awakening. Two days earlier she had been sitting in a casting office, awaiting her call, when she happened to really look at one woman who was coming out of the interview room. "She was younger than I was," Tanya said. "Definitely skinnier. Probably had more talent, too. But the reason I even noticed was that after she left, these young girls across the room started talking about her. They were laughing at her, really. Both of them saying they hoped they wouldn't be like her—some has-been theatre major still trying to become a movie star." Tanya closed her eyes, spilling more hot tears down her cheeks. "Hearing it put that way . . . I felt like I was looking into a mirror. That is *me*, you guys."

Tanya wiped her eyes and went on. "I didn't even stay. I just got in the car and drove back to the airport. Then, on the plane—" She choked on another sob, and I put my arm around her. Ships leaned in and patted Tanya's leg.

"On the plane," she continued, "I sat across from this mother with two kids, and the whole time, all she did was read to them, draw with them, do things to entertain them. And—I never did that. My kids always just seemed like an intrusion. When they acted up, I just shoved them off onto Preston. My whole world was me."

"Oh, Tanya, you were a good mother," Crystal said. Crystal is now a bishop's wife with six kids. She would probably pat a burglar on the back and say, "Tell me all about it."

Tanya looked up at her with a rueful smile. "No, I wasn't. And I was a horrible wife, too. I should have listened to Maxine and been more supportive of Preston."

"Hey, these things happen," Ships said. "Nobody is ever one hundred percent responsible."

"Yeah, don't beat yourself up," I said. "We all stumble, we fall, we grab hold of our friends—" I gestured to the five of us gathered around the table, "and we take another step forward."

Tanya hugged me back. "I know," she said. "And you guys could probably see the mistakes I was making, but you stood by me. I don't know what I'd do without my girlfriends."

"We're your temple escorts," Maxine chirped. "We'll walk with you all the way back to the celestial kingdom." It was funny hearing Maxine say this. She was closer to that journey than any of the rest of us, yet seemed the least worried about it.

"That's really what it's like," I said, cradling Tanya's cheek with my hand. "We're here to help each other. We get knocked down, and then we pull each other back up."

"But I feel so bad because I caused it all," Tanya whispered.

I sighed. I didn't honestly feel that I could argue with her. But I knew she didn't need to see my disapproval right now.

"Hey," I said, lifting her chin, "now you can go forward."

Tanya took a deep breath, then released it in a chattering sigh. "I guess so." She seemed unconvinced.

"You can still make it home," Crystal said.

"That's right," Maxine said. "We're all on the same ladder."

"But Preston's already remarried. The kids *love* her." Tanya shook her head. "I'll always be the one who brought them all so much pain—"

"You can turn it around," Ships said. "I mean, you can't reverse time, but you can start from today and be the way you really want to be. You're not locked in, Tanya."

"It's true," I said. "That's what Christ's Atonement is about. You see something you did that was wrong, and you change your heart. It's called repentance." I smiled encouragingly.

Tanya looked at me with the youngest eyes that showed the most vulnerability I had ever seen in an adult's face. "Do you think He can ever forgive me?"

We all hugged her then, and reminded her that Christ's forgiveness is for everyone. It had started as a bout of asthma, but became a testimony meeting. Each of us reached out and shared not only our love of Tanya, but our love for the Savior, and the sureness of our belief that Tanya could put her life back together.

Tanya went to freshen up in the ladies' room, and came back breathing fine and looking resolved. "I am going to turn over a new leaf," she announced.

"You're gonna quit acting?" Ships asked, incredulously.

"Oh, I practically have already," Tanya said. "You know, I never did pray about that. I wonder what answer I might have gotten." She snorted.

"There's nothing wrong with pursuing your own interests," Maxine pointed out. "You just need to set priorities."

Tanya took a drink of ice water. "You know, I started out with the idea that I would just do occasional community theatre. I intended to make sure it fit around family life. But then . . . these opportunities in L.A. kept coming up and . . . I guess I just couldn't resist the pull." She sighed.

"Hey," I said, not wanting her to slide back into despair. "When you do find your next husband, think how much better a wife you'll be now."

"Yeah," Crystal said. "You won't make the same mistakes again. You'll be a . . . an eight-cow wife."

Tanya laughed. "That's right. I'll be like you guys."

We all scoffed, but then I said, "Well, actually, we're *ten*-cow wives." Every one of us knew better, but we loved the confidence that title inspired. And thus we became *The Ten-Cow Wives' Club*. We never asked our husbands if they would agree on that price tag, but we liked it, so it stuck. It inspired healthy confidence in ourselves, we thought.

"Oh, I am so much the ten-cow wife," Ships chortled, slapping her hands on the table so hard that she jingled the silverware. "That man is going to hear all about this tonight."

That luncheon was also Tanya's moment of truth. After that, she finally devoted herself to the gospel, quit hoping to become famous, and gave her complete life over to helping her children.

Tanya's change of heart was wonderful to see. She began to spend nearly every day helping at the rehab center with Molly, and checked in with Ryan as often as possible. She studied her scriptures, and shared some of what she was learning with her kids. Though they resisted her at first, a few months convinced them that Tanya's change was for good, and her newfound interest in the gospel was too sincere to ignore. She became a counselor in Primary, and an office manager for an insurance agent.

"Who would have thought I could be organized?" Tanya said, tickled with her own progress. "All this time I never knew I had it in me!"

"The Lord blesses us with many talents we don't always find," Maxine said.

"And some, like precision marching, that we shouldn't find," Ships said, enjoying a laugh at herself.

Tanya even looked prettier. She told us how she now felt more peace than she had ever known, and couldn't thank us enough, for standing by her as her friends.

"Well, that's all going to change as soon as you lose that weight you've been working on for years," Ships teased. "You're getting too gorgeous and attracting too much attention."

Tanya laughed. "I think I've finally accepted my body," she said. "This is who I am, and what I weigh."

We all stared at her for a minute, then looked at each other, and then started clapping.

"You've done it," I said. "Good for you."

Tanya rolled her eyes at our applause. "Well, it helps to pray, I found out. And to listen." She raised her eyebrows, acknowledging how long it had taken her. "Slow learner."

I hugged her. I was glad that Tanya's life finally seemed to be coming together.

## Herbed Lamb Chops
### (Pork chops may be substituted)

1/2 cup balsamic vinegar
1/2 cup fresh basil, finely chopped
1/3 cup olive oil
1 green onion, chopped
2 Tablespoons maple syrup
1 Tablespoon lime juice
1/2 teaspoon dried oregano
8 loin or rib lamb chops, 1 inch thick

Ships came up with this one—or rather, Marco, the basil-and-oregano king, did. We all fell in love with it, and usually enjoy a creamy pasta on the side.

Combine all ingredients together in a large resealable bag to make a marinade. Add lamb chops, close bag, and marinate for 1 hour, or up to 24 hours, turning occasionally. Grill or broil at medium heat for 5–6 minutes per side. Brush with marinade as chops cook.

Serves 4.

# Epilogue

*That their hearts might be comforted, being knit together in love . . .*
Colossians 2:2

A year later, Molly was not only off drugs but finishing school, making grades to rival Crystal's kids. She had found a wonderful therapist who helped her work through her anger at her parents about the divorce, and to appreciate the blessings she did have, even if her life didn't match her dreams. She was taking dance and had transferred to Preston's ward so she could spend more time with her father, and she was making friends with a solid group of LDS girls whose influence was tremendous. Noleen turned out to be a wonderful stepmom, and even Tanya admitted Preston had picked a good replacement for her.

We all gathered in the audience for one of Molly's dance recitals. "She'd make a wonderful precision marcher," Ships whispered.

Tanya rolled her eyes, and pointed at Ships with the program rolled up like a baton. "You stay away from her," she said. "I can't afford those costumes."

Ships laughed, and we reminisced about the goofy clothes we had worn in junior high and high school. "Watch, though," I said. "Those platform shoes and bell-bottoms will come back."

"No way," the others said. "That was just a blip on the radar screen, and now it's gone forever."

I smiled. "Fashions go in cycles."

"Well, I'm never wearing them," Crystal said.

"Me neither," Ships agreed.

We joined pinkies in the middle of the row of seats, making a pinky promise that we would never again wear platform shoes and bell-bottom pants.

Ryan had switched high schools, and went to live with Preston's sister in Sacramento. He was doing much better, and finally seemed to be choosing good friends. After high school, he was planning to join the navy. Tanya was just thrilled that he would be finishing high school. We all hoped he would serve a mission, but knew we should leave that up to Ryan.

Just before he left for the naval base, we celebrated at a pricey steakhouse he loved. I looked around the table at our husbands, and calculated how long we'd all been friends—for almost twenty-five years. A quarter of a century of cheering each other on, telling each other off, crying over each other's dead pets, helping each other's kids with homework, comforting one another through health problems, financial losses, pride, disappointments, moving, sending out missionaries, even a divorce. *If this isn't a family, what is?*

Eventually, Tanya began dating again. Nearly every month she'd tell us another hilarious adventure from the world of single-hood, and we all sympathized with her crazy predicaments.

"You can't believe the guy I went out with this time," she would say, and then we'd sit back and let her tell us the latest horror story. "Flossed his teeth with fishing line—I swear—while we're sitting there in the restaurant!" Or when she dated a fellow actor, "His hair was a little long, but he said he was growing it out for a part. I figured, okay. But then I found out he had the same thing Samson had, only different. With this guy, as long as he doesn't cut his hair, he'll be stupid." Once at a party a guy came up to her and said, "My name is Don. As in Juan."

"For this I waste expensive perfume?" Tanya asked. We were gathered at her place for a luncheon—with our daughters, who, we had decided, were now old enough to appreciate linen napkins and heirloom china.

Molly, twenty-one now, just shook her head. "She knows she's sprayed enough perfume on when the dog starts rolling on the ground to cover himself with the scent."

Tanya laughed. "He does do that, come to think of it."

"Oh, I wasn't kidding," Molly laughed. I looked into her face and saw the little girl I had fallen in love with years earlier. It was so good to have her back.

Our daughters seemed to get a kick out of seeing us in the role of girlfriends, and thought our discussions were hilarious (whether you need to put on your blinker if you're in a turn-only lane, whether you can catch a cold by sitting on cement, whether men's and women's shirts should button from the same side, and whether we should do away with RSVPs since you can never get an accurate count anyway).

We reminisced about funny things that had happened on our excursions with the kids, and enjoyed seeing them squirm as we recalled the bird that bombed Hayley on the head in an open train ride through the redwoods, and the tanks of sea slugs that scared Ashley in Chinatown.

"Then there was the time you all went to the Jelly Belly factory without us," Ships said.

Francesca laughed. "I have to hear about this every time we pass Jelly Bellies in the store."

"We didn't go without you," I said.

"Yes, you did."

"We did?"

"I think we did," Crystal acknowledged. "First thing to go is your memory."

"Why weren't you there?" I asked.

"She had to renew her drivers' license," Tanya said. "Remember that?"

"Oh, hush up about my license," Ships said.

Now the girls all clamored to hear the story of Ships driving with an expired license and having a policeman give her a ticket and an ultimatum. The final day she could apply for renewal without getting a fine was the same day we had toured the factory.

"And so they went without me," Ships complained to the girls, trying to garner some sympathy.

"Good grief," I said. "Resenting us all these years. Would someone please give this woman a jelly bean?"

Tanya dug one out of her cake-decorating box, and threw it at Ships, hitting her in the back of the head.

"That is not funny," Ships said, pretending to be hurt.

"You've milked this jelly bean thing for long enough," Maxine said, waving away the whole show. "It's time you forgave us."

Our daughters all agreed, and Ships finally caved in. "But you owe me a tour," she said.

"How do you know we didn't take you on one, and you just forgot?" I asked. If I was going to lose my memory, I was certainly taking the rest of them with me.

Then we began to laugh at the sad realities of getting older.

"I already have a chin hair," Tanya said. "Two, in fact."

Crystal laughed. "I have to hold the phone book at arm's length so I can focus on it."

"That's nothing," Ships said. "I had to get a crown! My teeth are getting old!"

"I got a crown years ago," I said. "And the other night I got heartburn from eating too late."

The daughters were all grimacing, sure they would never get this ancient.

"You people are worried for nothing," Maxine said. "If I'd known how much fun it was to turn forty, I'd have done it twenty years sooner."

"But didn't you feel old?" Ashley asked.

"Oh, honey," Maxine smiled. "You just get hotter as you get older." All the girls shrieked with laughter and Maxine added, "Those aren't years—those are degrees in Fahrenheit."

We all laughed, and someone proposed that we go on a family cruise the year we all (except Maxine) would turn fifty. If we started saving now, we could probably do it.

"I just hope I'm still around to see it," Maxine said.

"Oh, you will be," we all chimed. Not one of us could believe she was already eighty-one.

Maxine winked. "True. I'll probably last another twenty-five years. Hey—maybe we can all get adjacent rooms at the rest home."

"Oh, what a thought," Tanya groaned. "Stuck with you guys in diapers?"

"Hey, you'll be wearing them, too," Molly reminded her mother.

"I hope I'll still have my teeth," Tanya said.

"You will," I told her. "Right beside your bed, in a jar."

We all groaned and decided that we were getting way ahead of ourselves.

"Oh, you've got lots of time before that," Maxine agreed. "You haven't even had a colonoscopy yet." The younger girls giggled.

"Last one in's a lucky duck," I mumbled.

Maxine laughed. "You think the mammogram years are tough."

"What is a mammogram, anyway?" Sydney asked.

"Honey, it's where they crank your breast flat between two metal plates, so they can x-ray it. Every mammogram feels like it takes a year off your life." The younger girls' eyes widened and Maxine laughed. "Believe it or not, women put up with this. Why don't one of you young smart things invent a better system?"

They nodded, obediently.

Maxine chuckled. "Aging is okay if you do it with friends. Although I am a bit ahead of you all."

"You've always been ahead of us all," Tanya said, and gave Maxine's shoulders a squeeze.

"You're the first ten-cow wife," I told her.

"I can almost hear Sam chuckling at that," Maxine said.

I looked at our daughters, and the admiration in their eyes as they listened to Maxine. How grateful I was for her presence in their lives, for the role model she truly was, as the greatest wife a man ever had.

\* \* \*

Four years later, Hayley graduated from BYU in business, and went to work with Jonathan. Dylan finished high school and began working for the parks system on weekends, trimming trees, gardening, and looking forward to having roommates, and living on his own. The bishop found a mission for him working for Deseret Industries, and Dylan was elated. He polished his missionary badge every morning, and wore it proudly as he took the bus to and from his work.

Crystal's oldest boys went on stateside missions, Ashley went to school majoring in chemistry, and the younger ones continued in the lower grades, a strong LDS family of temple-bound children.

Molly opened a dance studio, Ryan was in the navy, and Ships's kids were both married. Gino had become a dentist, and Francesca was expecting the first grandchild of the Ten-Cow Wives' Club.

We realized that the storms we had weathered had bound us irrevocably together. When crises arose, we didn't seem to feel the same panic we did in our earlier years; we knew we'd make it through with each other's help.

And then came the trial none of us wanted to face: Maxine died. Her heart just failed one winter night in her sleep, and she went home to reunite with Sam.

I got the call from Maxine's neighbor and visiting teacher, who checked on her every day. The entire ward and community were in shock. Maxine was everyone's secret idol, and somehow we had thought that made her immortal.

Jonathan dashed home from work and held me while I grieved. "How will I go on without her?" I asked. "She's been our . . . our guide."

"A lighthouse," Jonathan whispered, and I nodded.

The club gathered at my house, and we all hugged and cried. The weather was unseasonably sunny and bright for San Francisco, and we all decided Maxine had made it so.

That night as I was brushing my teeth, I realized: Maxine had never made it to Singapore. I called the girls, and we did her entire funeral in a Singapore theme—the flowers, the food—Maxine would have loved it.

Jonathan, Marco, and Peter all spoke at the funeral, praising her as an elect lady, and expressing their hopes that their daughters would turn out just like her. Jonathan cried unashamedly; he had really loved Maxine.

Tanya, Crystal, Ships, and I sat blubbering into Kleenex, knowing Maxine was in a better place, but still missing her deep in our bones. We made a second pact that day: we would try to be like Maxine, and earn our way back, like she did.

That night, three of Hayley's friends came by to offer their condolences and to bring her a beautiful Bird of Paradise bush and a plate of peanut-butter fudge. "You guys are the best," Hayley said, hugging them hard and wiping her tears.

I'd met them all before. Amber was a P.E. major engaged to a pre-med student, and Paige and Tiffany were both working at a local television station, and dating two fellows quite seriously. Only Hayley was unattached, reminding me of my own last-to-love status when I was her age.

They chatted comfortably, and Amber smoothed Hayley's blush where a tear had streaked her makeup. "You need us to keep you well groomed," Amber teased.

"I need you for a lot more than that," Hayley said. "I don't know what I'd do without you guys." Then, she turned to me and said, "Mom, this is my ten-cow wives' club."

"We just need to become wives now!" Paige laughed.

And so the mantle passed.

I smiled, watching the easy interchange between them. "You'll need wands," I said.

They all giggled and nodded. "Oh, yes—Hayley's taking care of that."

I kissed each of them on the cheek. "Be there for each other, no matter what," I said. "And know that wherever Maxine is, you've made her very happy."

# Peanut-Butter Fudge

14 ounces chocolate or vanilla chips, or candy
coating
1 (14-ounce) can sweetened condensed milk
Dash of salt
1/2 cup peanut butter
1/2 cup chopped peanuts, optional
1 1/2 teaspoons vanilla extract

This is a favorite of the new Ten-Cow Wives' Club.
I hear they eat it while they're studying for finals.

Line an 8-inch-square pan with waxed paper. In
heavy saucepan over low heat, melt candy coating
with milk and salt. Remove from heat. Stir in peanut
butter, then peanuts and vanilla. Spread evenly into
pan. Chill 2 hours or until firm. Turn fudge onto
cutting board, peel off paper, and cut into squares.
Store loosely covered at room temperature.

Makes 2 pounds of fudge.

## About the Author

Joni Hilton is the author of sixteen books, many published for the LDS market. She holds a master of fine arts degree in professional writing from USC, is an award-winning playwright, and is frequently published in major magazines. She is a weekly columnist for *Meridian* magazine (an online magazine for LDS readers) and is a writer for *Music and the Spoken Word.* A former TV talk show host in Los Angeles, Joni also travels to major TV markets as a spokesperson for various corporations. She has served as ward Relief Society president, first counselor in a stake Relief Society presidency, and currently serves as regional media consultant in the Sacramento Area where she lives. Many of her motivational-speaking tapes are also released by Covenant. She is the founder of Holy Cow cleaning products. She is married to Bob Hilton, and they are the parents of four children.

If you would like to be updated on Joni's newest releases or correspond with her, please send an e-mail to info@covenant-lds.com. You may also write to her in care of Covenant Communications, P.O. Box 416, American Fork, UT 84003-0416.

# Book Club Discussion Questions

1. How important are friends to women and to their growth in life? Do you have a group of friends similar to the Ten-Cow Wives' Club?

2. Are you still friends with girls you met in school? How are they different from your other friends?

3. Are you a ten-cow wife?

4. Of the women in your life, do you have a Maxine? Did she need to be older in order to be wiser?

5. Do you know any apparently "perfect" LDS families? Can you think of any struggles those families have had?

6. Did you find it difficult to like Tanya? How do you react when a friend or relative makes wrong choices?

7. Do you know any women who have had to come to grips with being unable to have children? How did they do it?

8. What do children with challenges bring to a family?

9. Can a woman mix career and motherhood?

10. Do you feel pressured to make your children compete and excel?

11. Can we blame the parents when the children don't turn out "right"?

12. Which are easier to raise—boys or girls?

13. Should friends always be absolutely honest with each other?

14. Does life get better as we age?

15. If fairies could bestow gifts, what gifts would you wish for your children?